The Brontë Sisters: A Room of Their Own

A collection of material inspired by the lives and works of the Brontë sisters
Edited by Nicola Friar

First Edition
ISBN 9798372274433

Title page illustration by Karen Arthur Neis
All other illustrations by Jess Tubby

A CIP catalogue record for this title is available from the British Library

Dedication

For three sisters.

And for Bob; always for Bob.
A lover of life, the Brontës, and Haworth who knows that I'm
just going to write because I cannot help it.

Acknowledgements

Without the writers who answered my call to arms yet again, this edition would not have been possible to produce. For further information on these individuals, please refer to this edition's "Contributors" section.

Thank you also to readers of *The Twelve Adventurers and Other Stories: A New Edition* and *The Bronës: Afterlife* whose feedback helped make this volume what it is.

Special thanks to Jess Tubby and Karen Arthur Neis for illustrating this volume.

Contents

Introduction

The Brontë sisters are three of the most famous writers in history. Against the odds in a nineteenth-century patriarchal society Charlotte (1816-1855), Emily (1818-1848), and Anne (1820-1849) produced poetry and bestselling novels that are still read and loved globally more than two centuries after their births.

The sisters' own written works reflect the struggles and trials of their contemporaries and continue to inspire new forms of art and literature in the twenty-first century. This collection comprises original material inspired by the sisters, the struggle for female freedom and space, and the celebration of women seeking a room of their own.

The sisters have inspired and influenced generations of women, writers, artists, and poets, and in doing so have forged connections between those who without their passion for the Brontës might perhaps never be brought together. It is fitting that this volume features a variety of contributors from different walks of life and nationalities, and with varying levels of writing experience, further demonstrating the power of the sisters' legacy. Although the struggle for female space continues, so does the celebration of women who have boldly gone before us and kept a candle burning for those who do not yet have a room of our own.

Nicola Friar
Glass Town, 2023

ﻌﻌﻌ

The Brontë Sisters: A Room of Their Own

Poetry

A Room of Their Own

By Maria van Mastrigt

Here I am, sitting in a room on my own.
Where are the others? Where do they roam?
Nothing at all happens, just an empty head!
What did our three sisters do, whenever they met?
In a room of their own, the stories they told,
Some of them gentle yet others were bold.
Did they suffer moments where nothing at all came?
Such a loss of great stories…oh what a shame!
I sit here and ponder, but nothing to write.
Perhaps this poem will do, perhaps it just might.

Emily's Room

By Debs Green-Jones

I'm the gloom of her room
On a raw afternoon
Alone in her room
As narrow as the tomb
As wide as a womb
By the light of the moon
She foresaw her own doom.
Who are we to presume
That we knew her.

In a Room of Her Own

By Alice Harling

In a room of her own she detailed maps of a new world;
a world with endless space, so many rooms -

But still, there was no room for her.

In that room of her own she dreamed of the right to room;
rooms for physicians, rooms for professors-

But still, she was barred from those rooms.

In one room of her own she described two rooms:
one a penitentiary, and one probationary-

But still, she could not escape her room.

In this room of her own she decided she was worthy;
of multiple rooms, a title and land -

But still, no one granted her more room.

In a room of her own she developed a fear of rooms;
gloomy schoolrooms, haunting sick-rooms-

But still, though she could never really leave her room;
her genius occupies boundless space, in so many rooms.

ھھھ

Short Stories

Breathing

By Naomi B.

The sky was turning pink. It was a smoky pink, a light one. It reminded her of a watercolour. It was a smooth tint to start the day with. She could hear her sister's footsteps in the kitchen downstairs. They were light, too, but firm and hasty. Her sister knew her morning tasks by heart; they were always the same. She would make bread with Tabby, then disappear outside or into her bedroom.

Anne closed her Bible and allowed herself a few more minutes of peace. Her thoughts went back, far into the past, to a face she would never see again. It had been nice to hope for quiet happiness. She remembered his smell and its freshness, his slow, still manners, and the way she would feel drawn to him. He was kind and God had been impatient to have him by His side. She was in love with a dead man. It was no use to deny it or to dwell on dreams.

She stood up, put her Bible back in the drawer of her desk and walked to the stairs as quietly as possible. Branwell was still asleep, she assumed. His night had been agitated; she had heard him speaking and screaming in his sleep again. She had also heard Emily whisper soothing words to him while carrying him to bed after she had brought him back home from the pub. Drunk. Again. Anne had helped her the night before, but Branwell had pushed her away and called her names. Emily said she would take care of him on her own from then on.

Anne went down the stairs and into the kitchen. Her sister was putting the bread into the oven and Tabby was making the tea. Emily looked tired. Her eyes were a bit swollen and she was thin. Anne was certain she had not gotten any sleep. She asked where Charlotte was. "In town" was the answer. Anne seized one of the cups Tabby had poured the tea into and took it to her father. The man did not like being interrupted in his studies; only Anne was quietly welcome to help him with his morning tea. She gently knocked at the door and waited for his answer. He allowed her to come in. She greeted him in a whisper, put the hot cup on his desk - always in the same corner - and left.

Back in the kitchen, Emily asked her how their father was. He was good, as always. Anne drank her tea in silence. Flossy suddenly ran to her, greeted her good morning with her tongue out and her tail agitated. She was excited and impatient to go out. Keeper followed, stepping into the kitchen slowly with a pigeon in his mouth.

"Oh, Keeper—" Anne sighed. She tried to seize the bird out of the dog's mouth, but he would not let her. Emily turned round and, without a word, firmly tapped his head. Keeper let go of the pigeon and it fell onto the kitchen floor. He looked up at Emily, hoping to be apologized **to**, but she was already focused on the cleaning of the kitchen. Flossy hurried to the bird and approached her nose to it, curious. Anne pushed her away while Tabby took up the poor dead pigeon in some linen and went to put it back outside where it belonged. Keeper would play with it later in the yard, or it would be stolen by some other animal or the wind.

The wind. Anne had a poem to complete, and a story to continue, but she suddenly felt the urge to go out. It was still early, the moor would be chilly, but she still fetched her coat and put it on. Flossy followed her and enthusiastically ran to the door. Anne informed her sister that she was going for a walk and left the house. She knew the shortest way to the moor; so did Flossy. Together they followed the path they had known forever.

Anne had been right - the wind was cold but pure. It was the end of autumn, that period in the year during which the weather and the hills seemed to hesitate between different temperatures, between various shades of colours. Flossy was running wild, her ears jumping up and down. She was breathing the wind, chasing butterflies. Anne smiled. She had arrived at the lonely parts of the moor, where she rarely met a soul.

She closed her eyes and the wind seemed to whisper a line or two to her. She regretted she had not brought her pencil and notebook; she would have to memorize them. When she opened her eyes again, the colours looked so bright to her. Some bushes were timid green, others openly purple. There was no limit above, no frontier between the hills and the sky, which was no longer pink, but slowly turning grey. A gigantic cloud was approaching, as though trying to gently stroke it. It had a strange hue, perhaps because it was made of several others. Anne could see dark blue, pink again, and light grey. She was standing inside a painting.

She kept going a little further, unwilling to feel locked in again. She liked the parsonage, the peace and quiet in it, and she loved the souls who inhabited it. But the wind was sometimes a song to her ears, a song that would call out her name. She could never resist it. She had missed it when she had been away, and she had been away for so long. It had felt like she had abandoned a piece of herself in the moors, a piece she had not been able to replace in York. But now she was back. For good.

Flossy barked at her, desperate to get her attention. Anne looked up. The colour of the cloud was slightly changed; it reminded her of Emily's eyes. She answered Flossy and pulled her skirts a little up to ease her way towards her. The dog had caught a crow. She dropped it at Anne's feet, expecting a reward. Anne sighed and stroked her behind the ears. She did not like it when her pet killed other animals but she was incapable of scolding her the way her sister did with her own dog.

They left the crow to the moor and kept walking, penetrating the painting even deeper. The horizon was endless; perhaps they had been there for hours, perhaps days. One could never tell. Time made no sense there. The moors had their own laws and followed no human schedule. Anne had to slow her pace. Her corset was making her breathing difficult and the weight of her dress made her sweat. In her slowed movements and breath, she found a rhythm she would later use in a poem. She felt inspired but they would have to go back soon.

Their way back to the house was quick. Flossy looked disappointed, but Anne was unyielding. She had to write. They arrived at the parsonage. Anne went into the dining room and held her hands to the fire. She had not realised it was so cold outside. Then she went straight upstairs to her bedroom, took out her notebook, ink, and pen, and went back down to the dining room. She sat down and immediately wrote down the lines she had in mind. After a few minutes, she dropped her pen and breathed out. It was as though she had not relaxed since the lines had entered her head. There they were. Written down. Safe. They could not get lost in her brain, or be forgotten in some dark place in her memory.

She read them again and then started some corrections. She would need Emily to read them too. She often required her sister's opinion. Anne knew she should be more confident about her work, yet poetry was pitiless. The story she had begun a few weeks ago felt more natural to weave. It was still a draft, and Anne did not know where it would lead exactly, but she could not stop writing it. Every time she would work on it, she felt something in her stomach loosen up. Her experiences as a governess had not always been easy and pleasant. Living away from her family and her favourite landscapes had been nearly traumatic. She had forced herself to keep going and never complain, but a mass had formed in her body, a mass of frustration and words. She had to release it.

Anne's pulse was quick. She had to calm down. She closed her eyes and appeased her breathing. It was noon when she opened them again and read her work for the tenth time. Suddenly, she heard a noise from upstairs. Branwell was getting up, probably lurching as something fell down and resonated in the dining room. Anne briskly closed her notebook - her brother did not know that the three sisters wrote - and gathered her things, ready to rush back up to her room and hide them there. But Branwell was going down the stairs, she could hear his unsure steps, and he barged into the dining room which looked so narrow suddenly. The daylight crossing the window pane made the look in his eyes even wilder. They were dark, his eyes, and damp. Wet with the drinks of the previous night.

Anne looked down. It was painful to see her brother lose control of himself so vehemently. Why could he not try at least? Why had he given in so easily? They all had lost companions who had been dear to their hearts; why was he the only one who was allowed to show it? And show it repeatedly.

"Morning, Anne."

"It's noon," she replied. Branwell staggered to the closest chair and sat down heavily, his body an immense burden. He sighed. Anne could smell his thick, foul breath from where she was standing. It was a hot, dizzying smell made of bitter beer, whiskey, and lack of hygiene. It reminded her of the day he was so drunk he vomited on his shirt and she had to wash him. Wash her own adult brother.

She turned her head. Branwell gazed at the yard through the window and she silently walked to the door, trying to escape. When she got near him, he caught her arm and told her he did not remember what he had done or said the night before. Anne did not reply; there was nothing to say. Every day, her brother would claim he had no recollection of his wrong deeds or hurtful words. None of his sisters believed him. Bad and good did not exist in a drunk's mind. Truth and lies were indistinct. Anne freed her arm and left the room.

Upstairs she left her things in her drawers and went back down to the kitchen to help her sister and Tabby with the daily chores. They asked her if Branwell was awake. They must have heard him. She said he was. Anne helped with the cooking and the sweeping. She hung up the laundry and helped Tabby set the table in the dining room. Branwell was standing at the fireplace now, contemplating the flames. He mumbled something and Anne thought she recognised a poem by Byron but she ignored him. She walked into the hall and knocked at the door of her father's study again. She told him lunch was ready. She always called him to meals before the food was actually on the table, for she knew her father would first finish whatever work he was doing before joining them in the dining room.

Anne took a seat at the dining table. She was hungry. She looked at Emily who was whispering to Branwell, his hand in hers, probably trying to convince him to have some food. She looked at Charlotte who had gotten back from errands and was helping Tabby fill the plates. And she looked at her brother who was clearly torturing their sister and expecting more pleading from her. And she thought of her father who had spent the entire morning in the quiet of his study, surrounded by books and not expected in the kitchen or anywhere else in the parsonage.

Emily was too patient with Branwell. He was the only person she was so forgiving with, for she knew he was weak. She would have been patient with her, too, perhaps. Yes, surely. But Anne had never had to challenge her sister's indulgence. Charlotte simply ignored him. She would sometimes look close to him, but her eyes would never stop on his actual figure. Anne knew Charlotte was hurt; she knew she would never understand such surrender.

They started lunch in silence. The soup was thick and nourishing, the bread Emily had made was tasty and light as the air. Their father did not look up once at them but asked Charlotte if the town was busy. Charlotte answered that it was not, people preferred to go out in the afternoon because the air was so fresh at the time she had left. Their father said fresh air was good for one's lungs. Charlotte did not answer. Anne asked her father what he was studying. He was reading psalms again to prepare for Sunday's sermon. Anne asked if he had found anything new in them. He said there was always something new to find in them.

Branwell abruptly got up, surprising his family, and left the room. Anne turned round to see where he was going and saw him seize his coat. They heard him open and then slam the door. He would not have done it on purpose; he had just left suddenly and had not thought to close the door behind him. Emily was staring at their father in her unperturbed way and asked him to forgive her brother. They finished their meal quietly.

Charlotte and Tabby cleared the table. Anne gently poked the fire. It was cold, and November was fierce. The room grew a little darker all of a sudden. Anne turned to the window to have a look at the weather. She noticed a flash of lightning. It had been abrupt and quick, but Emily had seen it too, and her grey eyes opened wide. She did not need to mention she was going out. Anne fetched her sister's coat and lent her her own gloves, for she had forgotten them in the morning and had regretted it. Emily thanked her with a smile and whistled at Keeper who was already at the door.

Anne knew her sister would be gone for hours, and she knew she did not need company other than Keeper's. She would often allow Anne to go along with her, and they liked each other's presence, but the promise of the thunder was a call to freedom Emily could not ignore. And freedom, to her, was a solitary place. Anne respected that, closed the door behind her and watched her sister and her dog head quietly for the moor. She thought they were great companions. Soul mates. She thought Keeper would be the first to hear the next lines Emily would write down later in the day. Or the following night.

Anne smiled. She turned around and realised she was alone in the room. Charlotte was probably upstairs, reading or writing; Tabby was certainly busy with her tasks; her father was back in his study, he would go for a walk in a few hours, once the sky would be clear; Branwell would not be home before the middle of the night, leaning all his weight against Emily's arm; and Flossy was playing outside. Anne felt crushed. Again, that corset. It was too tight, she thought. But it was also that room. Too small. And that dress, too heavy. And that wind. Sometimes, that wind would be too loud.

A Red Room of One's Own

By Tracy Neis

I marked the payment I had just made to the haberdasher in my late aunt's ledger and reminded myself not to fret over the expense. Surely it was no business of mine if my cousin Georgiana chose to dispense with the few funds remaining in the Reed estate so frivolously. Not a farthing of my family's vastly depleted fortune would be bestowed upon me, after all.

I moved my dip pen to the first column of the page and printed out the day's date in my neatest hand beside my latest notation. My heart began to race as I contemplated the passage of time. I had exceeded the fortnight that Mr Rochester had allotted for my absence by several weeks now. I feared he might have forgotten me.

And why should he not? taunted the voice of Reason in my head. *You are his employee and nothing more. When you return to Thornfield, the preparations for his impending wedding with miss ingram should be well underway. Cast off your foolish longings!*

I put down my pen, blotted the ink on the ledger, and stood up. I wondered if anyone would ever bother to read the record of accounts I had kept so carefully, at the request of my cousin Eliza, since my aunt's death. Robert, the coachman at Gateshead and the husband of my childhood nurse Bessie, had mentioned to me in passing that two distant relatives of my late Uncle Reed had filed separate claims to the estate.

One, a kinsman who hailed from Leeds, was more closely related to Georgiana, Eliza and me by blood, but he was the grandson of the daughter of Uncle Reed's aunt. The other claimant was a third cousin, once removed, who resided in Scotland and had never stepped foot inside England. But he was descended from our great-great-grandfather entirely through the male line, albeit through a series of youngest brothers. Robert suspected his claim to the land would win in court.

It seemed a small tragedy to me that neither Eliza nor Georgiana, who had lived at Gateshead their entire lives, could inherit the property they called home. I, of course, had spent the first ten years of my own existence residing within the confines of this grand estate as well. I knew its grounds far better than either of my warring, male relations. But I had never considered Gateshead my home, so I did not mourn its loss. Quite the contrary. I could hardly wait to leave this wretched place and return to my master at Thornfield.

I stepped into the hallway, climbed the tall, winding staircase, and approached my cousin Eliza's bedroom. I stood in front of her door and listened to her loud mutterings as she packed and repacked her earthly possessions. I considered knocking on the wood and telling her I had settled the accounts for the day, then thought better of it. I would probably see her at supper this evening and could give her a reckoning of the day's expenses then. After she finished her lengthy recital of prayers over our meal, that is.

I turned and walked the other way down the hall, but as I approached the Red Room, I hesitated. I had not stepped inside this foreboding chamber since the day my aunt had locked me inside its confines as a punishment for a crime I did not commit. A memory flashed before my inward eye of the light I had seen dancing along one of the chamber's walls that dreadful afternoon. With the passage of years, I had come to believe the mysterious light had been nothing but a rogue beam from a lantern one of the groundskeepers had been shining to light his way across the lawn on that dark day. At the time of my imprisonment, however, my childish self had been quite convinced that the light was my uncle's ghost, come back to haunt the bedroom in which he had died.

Did I wish to step inside this room once more, I asked myself, before I left Gateshead forever? I put my hand on the brass doorknob and considered. A quick glance around the chamber might put to rest any lingering fears I still harboured of my childhood home being haunted. I had made peace with my Aunt Reed on her deathbed a few weeks ago, after all, even though I had sworn my undying hatred to her eight years before. Perhaps my current, prolonged stay at −shire might indeed have been worth my time away from Mr Rochester if I returned to Thornfield with a lighter heart.

My fingers trembled as I squeezed the doorknob. A powerful sensation of anger coursed through me as memories of the day I had been locked inside this room rose unbidden to my consciousness. The face of my cousin John sneering at me as I was pulled away from him flashed before my eyes. The sound of my own childhood voice echoed through my mind:

"Unjust! Unjust!" I heard myself cry. Had I indeed shouted those words as I was dragged away from my incorrigible cousin? Or did my soul simply feel the unfairness of my plight so strongly at that young age that I remembered having hurled a verbal accusation at my captors that I had, in truth, merely uttered in my mind?

I inhaled a deep breath and held it for several seconds while I composed myself. That terrifying day had long since passed, I reminded myself. And the arrogant boy who had tormented me was long since dead. I had nothing to fear from this chamber. I twisted the brass knob and stepped inside the Red Room.

The strong scent of dust immediately overwhelmed me. I tucked my hand inside the left pocket of my skirt and pulled out a handkerchief to cover my nose. I briefly reprimanded myself for being remiss in my responsibilities. Eliza had charged me with overseeing the servants' work since Georgiana had left for London, and I had given each of the maids a list of daily tasks. But I had never assigned any of the staff to clean this room. I'd assumed that they dusted and aired out the deserted chamber once a week, just as they had always done when I resided here. I had been wrong. I must air out this room myself.

The long, red curtains hanging at each of the chamber's two windows had been drawn shut, so the room was quite dark. Guided by the light of a sconce that stood behind me in the hallway, I approached the closest window, tied back the curtains, and threw open the glass panes to let in some fresh air. I repeated my actions with the other window, then stepped into the middle of the room to examine the furnishings.

A fine layer of dust covered the tabletops and chairs, and a flurry of dust motes danced in the beams of sunlight that shone in through the newly opened windows. But the room did not appear as unattended as I had initially surmised. The wooden floor seemed clean, and the red curtains that surrounded the magnificent bed in the middle of the room did not look entirely unkempt. I stepped toward the bed and examined the dark red drapes that hung from the mahogany frame which enclosed the mattress. The lustre had faded from the once-plush damask, and a few holes in the fabric suggested the presence of moths in the room. But the overall effect of the chamber was one of general neglect rather than gloom.

I cast my eyes about the room, trying to remember precisely where I had collapsed in my fainting fit so many years before. I saw no indentations on the faded carpets that harkened back to my spell. I sat down on the white chair that stood beside the bed. The upholstery also showed signs of being moth-eaten in places, but the fabric was unstained. That should not have surprised me. If no one ever entered this room but the cleaning staff, then who could have left a mark on the white material?

Then I remembered that my aunt used to come inside this chamber on occasion. But why did she do so? I scanned the room, hoping to glean an answer. My eyes fell upon the tall, mahogany wardrobe. Of course, I recalled. She kept some of my uncle's private papers locked in one of those drawers!

I stood up, approached the wardrobe, and tugged at

each drawer. All but one of them opened readily. I pulled at the last drawer in frustration, then remembered that Eliza had given me the master keys to the house, so I could oversee its closing. I pulled the ring of keys from the right pocket of my skirt and tried each of the smaller fobs in the drawer's lock. After I inserted and twisted the fourth small key, the drawer sprung open. I smiled at my success, then pulled out the contents of the drawer and placed them on a tabletop closer to one of the windows so I could examine them in the light.

There were many diverse parchments that appeared to be of a legal nature. I glanced at the first paper, then set the whole pile aside to show Eliza tonight at dinner. Perhaps she might want to share the briefs with the solicitor handling the transfer of Gateshead to its future owner. Then I spied a bundle of letters tied together with a pale ribbon. I undid the knot and spread the papers across the table. They appeared to be written in a woman's hand. I opened the one closest to me, inspected the name written at the bottom of the page, and began to tremble. The epistle had been written by my mother!

My heart raced as I gathered each of the notes together in my hands. I clutched the small treasure to my breast, hardly knowing what emotions I was feeling. I had no memories of either my mother or father. They had both died of typhus fever when I was but a babe. I sensed tears coming to my eyes, then blinked them away. This was no time for weeping, I chided myself. Read anon! This discovery alone had made my time away from Thornfield a precious undertaking!

With unsteady feet, I returned to the white chair and sat down. I sorted the letters by their dates, then began to read the missives my mother had sent to her brother, beginning with her note announcing her marriage to my father. She enumerated her husband's many good qualities in the most effusive terms. In subsequent letters, she showed considerable irritation at her dying father for writing her out of his will for marrying a poor clergyman. Then she wrote of her joy when she discovered she was with child and described my infant self in the most loving of words. I could not help but smile as I read her account of the insatiably curious nature and infectious, burbling laugh I displayed in my first few months.

The tone of her letters only grew dark when she informed my uncle of my father's illness and rapid decline. In her final letter, she wrote of her husband's death and her own symptoms that mirrored those he had shown before he died. She begged her brother to look after me in the event of her death.

What Uncle Reed replied to these letters I can only surmise. But I felt a sudden surge of gratitude to him for bringing me to Gateshead — undoubtedly against the wishes of his wife. This house had been no home for me when I was a child. After my Uncle Reed's passing, my aunt insisted that I always be treated as a poor relation. But after reading these letters, I became convinced that had my uncle lived, he would have treated me with the kindness my mother had urged him to show me. I re-read the final letter one more time, then rested the small pile of correspondence on top of the bed.

I examined the fawn-coloured walls and tried to remember the precise spot where I had seen the flash of light on that dreadful day eight years ago. Perhaps the light had been a sign from my uncle, after all, I postulated. His spirit might have been trying to comfort me in my hour of need, rather than terrify me further in my bleakest moments of despair.

I closed my eyes and let the joy of my newfound discovery wash over me afresh. A soft breeze blew in from the open window behind me, rustling the letters on the bed in front of me. I considered moving the pile of correspondence to another spot, outside of the wind's path, but promptly decided that action could wait. I shall enjoy my bliss, I declared to myself. Such moments of joy come rarely enough to me. Let me savour this. A powerful sensation of comfort enveloped me, and I felt myself falling asleep.

"Rest you, my daughter," whispered a voice on the

wind. I started at the sound and began to open my eyes. "No, sweet child," the voice continued. "Sleep, so I can speak to you."

I shivered as the breeze grew stronger. "Mother, is that you?" I whispered in my head, hoping the mysterious voice could hear me.

"Sleep, child, and do not try to converse with me," the voice replied. "Know only that I love you, and want all good things for you."

The hairs on the back of my neck bristled as the breeze disturbed them, but I kept my eyes shut, as directed. Surely, this must be a delusion of fancy, I told myself. A waking dream, brought on by a rare combination of unspoken wishes, unforeseen surprises, and physical exhaustion playing tricks on my mind. But the illusion pleased me immeasurably, so I indulged the voice and remained silent.

"Listen to me, Jane," the voice continued. "I do not know when I shall be able to speak to you again. But I am here now. You have read my letters to my brother. You know now that I loved your father with a reckless passion and gave up my share of our family's fortune for him. Our time together was achingly brief and ultimately doomed. But I have had years now to ponder the wisdom of my choice.

Your father and I turned our backs on our families so that we might better dedicate ourselves to Christ. But you did not make this choice. We foisted it upon you. As I lay dying, I asked my brother to care for you as his own daughter. I trusted in his kindness. But I did not consider the true nature of his wife, who always despised me. I should have known that she was in no way fit to be your guardian. I should have sought help from your father's brother, John Eyre, instead."

"John Eyre," I mumbled under my breath. The name sounded familiar. Had my Aunt Reed mentioned him to me before she died?

"Hush, child," the voice urged me again. "Do not attempt to speak, lest your wakeful self overpowers your peaceful rest, and break the fragile bond that now unites our hearts like a taught string. You have heard the name John Eyre of late, I believe. My sister-in-law spoke to you of him. You must seek him out. He has money. You need money. He can offer you protection. You need protection."

Why did I need protection? I wanted to ask the voice. My life held few prospects, to be sure, but I was in no imminent danger. I was an educated woman. I was gainfully employed. I was even in possession of a strong hope that Mr Rochester loved…

"Seek out your Uncle John Eyre!" the voice reiterated, interrupting my thoughts. "You are a woman alone in this world, and men will try to take advantage of you. Your uncle can care for you and keep you safe from unscrupulous men."

Men! I thought, a sudden wave of anger surging through me and bursting my bubble of bliss. Men hold all the power in this world and all of the rights! My cousin John inherited his father's fortune yet dragged his mother and sisters into ruin along with him. And now my distant male cousins from Scotland and Leeds will be taking what's left of this estate from my female cousins, who in all fairness ought to have inherited the land. A man of the cloth who possessed no sense of godliness or compassion wreaked havoc on the girls' school I attended as a child and tried to snuff the life out of me and my fellow female students. Through his reckless neglect of the responsibilities he had assumed, Mr Brocklehurst killed my dearest friend. Why, there is only one truly good man in this world that I have ever met! And I cannot wait to return to him!

I opened my eyes, feeling suddenly wide awake, and noticed that the room had grown darker. I must have slept for an hour or more. I let my eyes adjust to the pale light of the receding sun, then examined my surroundings. The letters I had placed on the bed were gone.

I jumped from my chair and frantically searched for them. I found one letter tucked inside a fold in the curtains hanging over the mattress. I found another on the floor on the other side of the room. I felt a chill pass through me and realized I needed to close the windows. I clutched the two letters I had retrieved to my breast and sighed. I would have to return to this room in the morn to collect the remaining missives. It was too dark for me to find them now.

As I approached the first window and reached for the handles to shut the panes, I tried to remember the dream I had just had. It had been wonderful, I recollected, but its details were already beginning to fade from my memory. Had I dreamed of my mother? Or of my uncle? Which uncle — my Uncle Reed or my Uncle Eyre? I could not think clearly with my emotions running so freely.

I walked to the second window and started to close the panes, then noticed one of the letters resting on the sill. I reached for it but knocked it out the window by mistake. A wave of anger flooded me. I wished I could curse aloud like Mr Rochester did with such frequency and without compunction.

"Jane, is that you in there?" came a voice behind me. It didn't sound soothing like the voice which had lulled me to sleep. It sounded like my cousin Eliza. "Jane, step out of this room at once!" the voice chided me. "This is where my father died. No one is allowed inside this room. Don't you remember that? Now, come and join me for dinner. Cook has prepared our last hen. We mustn't keep her waiting."

I closed the window and straightened my shoulders. As I turned toward my cousin, I noticed the light from the sconce in the hallway was shining through the doorway, casting her figure in silhouette and brightly illuminating the entrance to the Red Room. The rest of the chamber seemed all the more obscured by shadow in contrast. I would find no further letters tonight. I walked to my cousin's side and offered her a small nod as I joined her in the hallway. She continued with her scolding lecture, but I ignored her, plotting instead how I might get my hands on the letter that had fallen out the window before night fell completely, and the world became dark once more.

A Withens Tale

By Rebekah Clayton

I tell thee, it were bitter that January. The day started fine -
cold, blue skies an' Stanbury Moor hoary wi' a cracklin' frost.
Silvery needles of ice stiffened every sprig of heather and tuft
of sedge. Bonny enough, I grant you, though I grumbled as I
trudged t' well, shielding my eyes from the glare off Delf Hill
and Withens Height.

The spring water still babbled, trickling o'er stone,
through ice and fern, down into a rough trough. I broke the
surface with my pail and filled it to the brim. The cows in't
mistal [1], an Nelly our pig, an the geese and yows hurdled in't
laithe [2] porch, needed water and fodder, however cold it got.
And we needed our hot tea and porridge, and to wash an'
comb the fleece ready for weaving.

You know, it's funny to think on't, but we knew them,
we knew *her*, long before they were famous; before the whole
world came t'Haworth. Jonas, my husband, remembered them
as children - all six of them, coming up t' farm. Like little dolls
they were, he said - small and pale as porcelain, wi' big, big
eyes, holdin' hands wi' young Sarah Garrs. They might bide
awhile on warm summer afternoons and take a cup of the ice-
cold spring water and a morsel of oatcake, hot off the bake-
stone.

Later on, after we were wed (Jonas a fair stripling and
myself a rosy-cheeked wench), when Withens became my
home, I come to know them too; grave, young women –
learned, well-spoken, and dainty-like. At least Charlotte and
Anne were, but she, *she* wor different - tall and graceful, an'
allus silent.

I would invite them in, proud to have such grand folk
visiting. Imagine! T'Parson's daughters!

"Miss Brontë," I would say, "step in for a cup 'o tea.
Kettle's on. What a gradly afternoon."

"That's very kind, but no thank you, Mary," Miss Charlotte might say. "Tabby will have our tea waiting for us at home."

It was always Charlotte who spoke. Anne might smile, but Emily's gaze was always on the horizon or her face hidden by her dark locks, as she bent down to scratch the sow's back, or fuss the farm dogs.

Occasionally, if the sisters were caught by a sudden shower or the roaring wind, they would step over the threshold and into the housebody. I would draw up chairs before the fire, clucking with pride, and give them fresh mashed tea or hot milk.

If Mr Branwell was with them (Brany they called him) the girls would stay quiet and he would fill the room with such chatter. Ee! I niver heard the like. Jonas and Feyther would stop their work just to listen. T'were like a magic lantern show: all lights, an' gasps, an' dazzle, and colour. Folks thought he wor summat special, that Branwell, but, after all, it were those lasses, so mousy and ladylike, that made the world sit up.

Emily niver said owt. Not then. Not until that bitter, beautiful day. As still as frozen water it were - until noontide, that is, and then we could feel it in the air, something gathering. The clear sky gave way to a sullen, heavy light, yellowish and strange - "ower-kessen" as we say. An' we knew what was coming.

Jonas and the dogs brought in the rest of the sheep, then he saw t'cows in New Laithe. I fetched and carried enough water to see us through. Feyther checked all doors an' windows and shut the pig in't sty. And John, my bonny bairn, barely four, drove the poultry into their hut. And we all carried extra turf from the peat house and stacked it high in the back kitchen.

We knew what were brewing on the horizon. We could see a girt, sickly shadow approaching. With the first flakes of snow, spiralling an' dizzy, in that biting wind, we retreated to the cosy, firelit interior, to spin and weave and weave and spin, safe in the path of the winter storm.

So, we wor fair staggered when came a loud knocking. Wor it t' wind gusting hard agin the front door? But Pit and Ty, the shepherd dogs, were up, barking, fit to wake the dead.

"Lie down!" said Jonas. At once the dogs were still: crouched, tense. The knock came again, more urgent.

"Hearken," said Feyther.

"Tis a lost sowl. Mebbe it's thy Mither come yam [3]?"

John piped up, clutching at my skirts, his eyes round with fear, "Is it Gramma? O' Ma, is it us Gramma?"

"Nay, lad," I hushed.

"Yer Grandsah's jus coddin."

"Gi'o'er, Da," said Jonas, moving to the door.

"Well, tha knaws ah've seen 'er," Feyther muttered. "E'en a boggard [4] wants a wahm hearthstun." He were teasing, I'm sure. But on that wild, dark afternoon his words shook us all, more than we'd like to say.

Another outbreak of knocking. Jonas shot back the bolts and pulled the door open. A bitter blast howled in, and a figure, tightly wrapped against the cold, stumbled o'er the doorstones. I recognised the dog, a powerful beast, who shook the snow from his tawny coat. In an instance Pit and Ty were up, hackles raised. From the throat of the intruder came a menacing rumble.

A sudden command. "Keeper, down!"

Jonas slammed the board shut. "I'll put dogs in't laithe," he said and, giving a sharp whistle, ordered our collies through the inner door. Keeper lay low and the visitor unwound the muffler and doffed a thick felt hat.

"Why," exclaimed Jonas. "Of all folk!"

"Miss Emily," I said, stepping forward. "Jonas forgets himself. Tha mun be starved. Gi' me your coat and those wet things." I hung them by the door.

Jonas was still agog. "What brings you so far, Miss, i' this weather?"

"Might I stay?" she asked. She had this odd way of not looking at you.

"Child," said Feyther, rising from his chair, "sit thysen b'fire."

"I can't take your seat, Mr Sutherland," she said, a little stiffly.

"Nay," Feyther insisted. "Sit thysen dahn, lass. What possessed thee to be aht i' this snow-stoor?" Emily sat on the rocking chair and Keeper settled at her feet. Her face, I remember, was as pale as milk.

"I misjudged," she said and gave an odd smile. "I should have turned back. I could see it coming over the tops, but–" And suddenly her gaze was far away and there was a strange light in her eye. I had never heard her say so much.

"They'll be fretting at the Parsonage," I said softly. "Did they know you were headed this way?"

Emily nodded. "Yes and I passed Tom Pighills, the groom at Ponden, out riding. I *should* get back, but the paths will be covered. Perhaps Keeper could find the way."

Feyther gave a sudden gruff laugh. "Yow'll be lucky! Not wi' stowering this bad." And, as if in agreement, several flurries of snowflakes rattled hard against the window panes.

"Tha mun stay," said Jonas.

"It'll be days," said Feyther, shaking his head. "We'll be all happed-in."

*

Of course, he were raight. You can't live on top o' world all your life, like Jonas and his Da, an not know weather when you see it. T'were my job to get Miss Emily settled.

"You'll have your own room, that goes without saying."

"Please, don't trouble. I can sleep in a chair by the fire."

"Nonsense, Miss," I scoffed.

I set Feyther and John to fetch fleeces from the garret and blankets from the chest, an' directed them to make up a pallet in the parlour chamber, where Jonas had the second loom. I took her up the stairs to the house chamber. This was where Jonas and I, and Da and the bairn slept, and where Feyther had his master loom.

"It's just off here," I said, opening the dividing door.

Emily, who had been stiff and white, actually smiled – almost laughed – when she saw her room. "Oh, it's perfect!" she said. She moved to the wide mullioned window, with its five lattices, and gazed out at the wild tempest raging o'er the hills. "Perfect," she sighed. There was a pause, and then, "Might I have Keeper with me?" For a moment her dark eyes met mine.

We don't let dogs in the house, as a rule, and never upstairs. But, I could sense her need.

"Yes, Miss. I can see he's a good creature."

"And a candle?" She thrust her hand into her skirt pocket, withdrawing a silver threepence. I hesitated. Tallow was costly and though we had candles they were rarely used. We preferred rushlights.

"You're all right, Miss," I said, a little proudly perhaps. "We can spare a candle."

When I told Jonas, he said "'Appen she's afeared of dark?" But that weren't it. At night I could hear a faint scritch-scratchin', like a mouse gnawing through sackcloth. And a gleam of light flickered under the chamber door.

*

In the morning she was late to rise.

"Owd sleepy 'ead!" teased Feyther. "Tha' 'as ter rise sharpish wi' beasts t' feed." Emily half-smiled and joined us at breakfast: a great dish of steaming waff [5] was set in the centre of the table.

"I was up early, watching the storm," she said eagerly. "It's coming straight down the moor!"

"Aye, tis blowin' keen, an' ah must clear the paths," said Jonas, plunging his spoon into the waff and dipping it

45

into his mess pot. Emily watched him and inspected the blue-milky contents of her mug.

"Dunna fret abaht New Laith," said Feyther. "T'owd coos'll not yield, tis that nithering [6]," then, turning to Emily, "eat up, lass, afore it's all gone."

She picked up her spoon and cautiously scooped a portion of hot porridge from the common bowl.

"Dip it in, lass, dip it in," cried Feyther. "Like this." He thrust his spoon into the steaming waff, dipped it into his skim and gulped it down. "Yah mun put some meat o' them bones if yow're to graft."

Vaguely Emily dipped the spoon into her milk and said, "I'd like to work."

"Feyther," I scolded, "You can't expect Miss Emily–"

"I'd like to," she said firmly and, as Feyther chuckled into his pot, she swallowed her spoonful.

*

She was as good as her word. She helped me to clear away and wash the pots, brush the hearth, stoke up the fire and sweep through the house, with young John laiking [7] at our heels. Overhead we could hear the rhythmic clack-clack of Feyther's loom.

In the dairy, I showed her how to skim off cream wi' a skenk [8] and churn the butter. She enjoyed this task: her arms were thin but strong. Then we washed and beat and salted the butter and stored it in stone jars. Soon it was time for dinner. John curled up on the hearth-rug next to Keeper and played with his wooden soldiers.

"Can you mek oat cakes?" I asked, leading her to the back kitchen.

"I've watched Tabby do it," she said, uncertainly.

I set a fire beneath the bake-stone then took the bowl of fermented batter, added a handful of fine oatmeal, beat it and poured a dollop onto the riddle-board.

"See now, this is the tricky bit. You 'ave to reel it round, slip cake ont' damp spittle [9], then flip it on t' hot stone. Like this, see?" The batter sizzled on the bake-stone. "Then, when the edges curl, turn it o'er." She nodded, her eyes eager and alert. "Now, hang that one on't fleak [10] and you have a go."

She picked it up in no time and soon the house was filled with the fragrant scent of hot oatcakes.

"Mek eight," I said, "that'll do us, and we'll have some fried bacon and toasted cheese."

"Mary," she asked suddenly.

"Does anyone else live here?"

"What, Miss?"

"I saw someone last night, sitting by the fire. I thought it was you."

"Last night, Miss?" I cried.

"But we were all abed."

"I came downstairs, for some water. Someone was sitting in Mr Sutherland's chair. A woman."

Despite the heat from the bakestone, I felt a sudden chill. "You must ha' been dreaming, Miss!"

"No. Keeper saw her too. I felt his hackles rise."

I shivered. A voice came from the doorway.

"'Appen tha's seen 'er too, then lass." It was Feyther, drawn by the smell of cooking. "Ah've seen 'er mony a neet, lookin' through lattice, ah't ont' moor, sittin' i' that chair. My Annie. She wor a good woman."

"O' don't, Da," I said.

"We're dismal enough without conjuring up ghosts. Think on't bairn." I nodded towards John.

Feyther withdrew, but I could hear him singing, low - "Twas far in the night, and the bairnies grat, The mither beneath the mools heard that -"

I hurried after him, muttering that I must cut the bacon slices. I'm not superstitious, as a rule, but talk o' the dead unnerves me. Jonas came in not long after, shaking wi' cold, and reported that the snow was as high as his shoulder. We all gathered close to the fire to eat dinner.

*

After the meal, Emily asked if she could be excused and, wi' Keeper at her heels, ascended the stairs.

"Ah'll be mekkin a raight rattle wi' loom," Feyther called up after her. "If yow're wanting a nap."

"Oh no," she replied. "I won't be sleeping."

Jonas settled down to wool combing and I sat spinning and the sound of Da's loom clacked and clattered above our heads.

"She's a strange 'un," said Jonas.

"Aye," I agreed. "But a canny lass."

"Ah wonder what shoo's up to?"

*

Time passed and niver a sound came from her room. As the clock struck four, I mashed the tea, then climbed the stairs.

"Tea-time, is it?" said Da, as I appeared. "Ah can barely si' t' fettle [11]."

I knocked on Emily's door, opened it and peeped in. She hurriedly pushed something under the fleece and turned to me. She was wrapped in the blanket.

"Come and get wahm, Miss," I said. "I've brewed some tea."

"Thank you, Mary." She shed her blanket and stood up, then gazing out of the window said, "the wind is dropping, and the sky is clearing. I think there will be a moon tonight. It will be so beautiful." And half-dreamily she murmured, 'The chill, chill whiteness covers all -'" Her gaze lingered on the winter twilight.

"Come, Miss, you're shivering."

*

That evening after supper John climbed onto his grandsire's

knee and begged for a story.

"Ee, tha does claver [12], lad," grumbled Da, but he petted the bairn's head.

"Please do, Mr Sutherland," said Emily. So Feyther told us the story of poor Elizabeth Heaton who was seduced by a drunken scoundrel and forced into a shameful marriage and who, two year thence, thin and neglected, returned to Ponden with her baby girl, to die of a consumption.

"I remember that neet i' March, nigh on twenty year since," said Da. "Ah wor mekkin an urgent delivery of cream an' eggs f' ailing lass: they wor trying to build 'er up wi' rich vittals. But t'were too late. I saw through gloom, passing by garden, a ghostly lantern, carried by a grizzled owd man. She wor done for. T'were the sign of doom f' Heatons. Owd Greybeard, herald of death, folk call 'im. Poor Elizabeth died the next day, and, within ten month, her mother and her bairn wor dead too."

That night I heard the scratchy-scratchin' sound and saw that dim gleam flickering under the chamber door. It must a' been well past midnight before the light went out.

*

Next morning, after helping me to milk the cows and carry brimming pails to the dairy, Emily offered to help Jonas clear the snow. I took my chance. With brush and pan in hand, I entered her room.

"A' tha nebbin?" chuckled Feyther.

I gave the floor a few half-hearted sweeps, then went o'er to the fleece pallet and rummaged beneath. I drew out a penny notebook, into which was tucked the stub of a pencil. Inside, the pages were covered with cramped handwriting. Some scribbled down and some set out like the verses and ballads you sometimes see in news sheets. I could just mek out some lines.

*"My fingers closed on the fingers of a little, ice-cold hand! The
intense horror of nightmare came over me: I tried to draw back my
arm, but the hand clung to it, and a most melancholy voice sobbed,
"let me in – let me in!"*

I shuddered and stopped reading. I'd had enough of boggards
and spirits! I turned to the verses. The close scrawl was almost
impossible to read, but I persevered, my heart beating wildly:

*the shrieking wind sank mute and mild,
The smothering snow-clouds rolled away;
And cold – how cold!– wan moonlight smiled –*

And another.

*the night is darkening round me,
The wild winds coldly blow;
But a tyrant spell has bound me
And I cannot, cannot go.*

*The giant trees are bending
Their bare boughs weighed with snow,
And the storm is fast descending
And yet I cannot go.*

"Weel, A' niver," I breathed, sitting back on my heels.
Ah wasn't much of a scholar, but these words made me ache
inside wi' their lovliness. My hands were trembling. To think,
that silent girl had such a pure, uplifting voice.

I could hear Emily outside, calling Keeper and
laughing. I returned the notebook to its hiding place and,
standing up, leaned on the stone sill and peered through the
window. The world outside was white and Emily, shovel in
one hand, was throwing snowballs for the dogs and laughin'
and laughin'.

Sometimes, all these years later, wi' Emily and her

sisters long dead, I look around this humble chamber, wi' its loom and its view up t'moors and down o'er South Dean Vale, and I think o' the name of Bell, an' of Brontë, famous all o'er the world, mebbe. I remember that winter long ago; the little light flickering and the scratchin' of her pencil, and reflect on how her poetry – the poetry she wrote *here in this very room* – made me ache, ache inside, wi' its lovliness.

❧❧❧

[1] Byre or stall in barn
[2] Barn
[3] Home
[4] Ghost or malign spirit
[5] Porridge made with bacon fat
[6] Freezing cold
[7] Playing
[8] Dish
[9] Wooden board covered with damp cloth, used to flip oatcakes
[10] Rack to dry oatcakes
[11] Work
[12] Chatter

Of Love and Sorrow

By Tess Bentley

O, that lone flower recalled to me
My happy childhood's hours
When bluebells seemed like fairy gifts
A prize among the flowers
- Anne Brontë

1846

When I close my eyes and all is still, I can keenly recall the
sweet scent of heather as I used to lay happily in the grass as a
child. How glad I was then when my worries were few and all
my confidence lay deep in the bosom of my mother. My life
seemed simple. The days blended into each other. After my
lessons were complete for the day and my books were tucked
neatly away, I would grab my bonnet, pencil, and my drawing
pad, and make my way out to the moors.

Drawing was my first love. I spent many hours
observing the swaying heather and anticipating the coming
rain — attempting to capture a summer storm as it appeared
on the horizon. Mama and Papa praised my efforts and
proudly displayed my tiny drawings in the parlour for guests
to see. For my part, the effort was not in the task itself, but in
the intricate ways in which I tried to capture the moors. I
could never seem to create the picture I saw in front of me;
therefore, I was always a little deflated, despite my mama and
papa's praise.

One cool, late spring day, I did what I could to capture
the dying sun, spending far too long outside according to
Mama, when I returned home to a happy parlour. Waiting for
me was a pretty cake with white frosting and a small gift,
wrapped in brown parchment paper. I hadn't reminded mama
of my birthday this year as times were hard and I preferred
they worried about more important things.

"My darling Clara," Mama stated as she took me in her arms. "You are home rather late. I was beginning to worry - I could only keep your papa from your cake for so long."

I smiled at my mother and glanced over at Papa. I knew exactly how he looked before my eyes settled on his. He was sitting in his old wooden chair with dark leather, smoking his pipe. I never had to guess when Papa was home, for the parlour smelt of his Cuban tobacco.

"I'm sorry, Mama," I replied. I then handed her my newest drawing. "No matter how I try, I simply cannot draw what I feel."

With a kiss on the cheek, my mother stated, "Well now, it is often difficult to portray our feelings in the art we create, and yet, we still work towards that elusive goal."

"That is why you still write poems then mama?"

My mother stopped cutting my cake and glanced up at me. Her golden hair seemed like a halo around her face as the firelight bounced off her pleated crown. She gave me a small smile. My father, who had been a mere spectator, put down his pipe, stood up, and walked to the table. I watched as he pulled my mother into his large arms and kissed her softly on the head.

"Clara, darling, your mother has always had the heart of an artist. You use your pencil to put your feelings into pictures, your mother uses her pen to put her feelings into words. The two of you are cut from the same lovely cloth."

"Yes, Papa." My cheeks burned at being compared to my mother. If only I were so like her.

"Now, take that plate from your mother's hand and take this parcel from mine."

I laughed lightly as I had a prized possession in both of my small hands - how lucky I was!

"It's not every day that my only child turns ten. Be merry daughter and open your gift!"

Once I set the citrus-scented loaf down, I carefully unwrapped the brown paper, revealing a small book of poems. The dark leather was pressed, with a floral pattern border and a design, almost like a cello in the centre. It was the most exquisite little thing I had ever seen. I turned it as a ran my fingertips across the imprint and saw the title on its spine - *Poems* by Currer, Ellis, and Acton Bell.

"You like their work, Mama?" I asked. She was watching me closely.

"Well, my love, I haven't actually read anything from the Bell brothers before. I happened upon this little book when I was in town, and it was such a lovely little book I read a few of the poems to see if you would like them. I found them unique, quite unique. I thought we could read it together."

I ran to my mother and father and gave them both a kiss on the cheek. I told them how glad I was to have mother read with me. Every evening, after I came home from the moors, and after my evening toilette, I sat down with my mama, and we took turns reading from the little book of poems. Papa listened quietly. We each had our preference for one of the Bell brothers. Papa enjoyed the poetry from Acton, saying the words stayed deep in his spirit for days after he heard them.

For Mama, she mentioned that it was Ellis who held her attention most. When I asked her why she told me she didn't quite understand it herself. As for me, Currer's words had made an impression deep within my soul. That fire and passion! I read his lines over and over again. I thanked Mama many times over for my little book of poems.

As I found myself sketching the dying sun towards the end of summer, in my notebook were also a few poems written with my own pencil. I freely laughed, as only a child could do, for I then realised, I could draw better because I now understood how to connect my feelings to both drawings and words. Never again did I leave those moors frustrated at my ability to capture my thoughts and feelings on the paper in front of me.

*

Some have won a wild delight,
By daring wilder sorrow;
Could I gain thy love to-night,
I'd hazard death to-morrow –
Charlotte Brontë

1852

At ten years old, I was mesmerized by the moors. I thought them magical. At sixteen, my love had all but waxed cold. It was not the beauty of the land that my pencil ceased to find inspiration. The words — those that once came so rapidly to me — felt empty.

As I lay there, watching the summer sun wain, I should have been content. It wasn't so. I felt restless and with each day it grew. It was as if I had a battle brewing within me; the child enjoying her comforts and the woman seeking independence from all she knew. I wanted to see more of the world in which I belonged. Often, I imagined what the heat must feel like in the Mediterranean, and what of the sophistication of the Parisian ladies? Oh, to go to the theatre. And London! What I would give to see the city, my nation's capital. I knew that London was a possibility. I even asked my father if I could visit some of his friends there. The conversation left me with little hope.

"My darling girl, why do you wish to leave home so soon? We have a comfortable life here. London — well it's no place for a young lass such as yourself to dwell."

"Papa," I took his large hand, which was slightly calloused from age into mine. "Many young ladies spend a season in London. And you have cousins there — many cousins, who would be glad to have me. Remember? Cousin Tilly said she would be more than happy to receive me, even if it was for a few weeks."

My papa squeezed my hand before kissing it. I couldn't suppress a smile when I felt his thick beard tickle the top of my hand.

"Clara Jane," he began, just as he always did to soften bad news, "I know you are young and spirited. You see, those qualities that lift you up in my eyes above all other girls, are the very qualities that make me fear you leaving home so soon. Just hold on now and let me finish."

I sat down, placing my hands in my lap as he recommenced his thoughts.

"You are able to come and go as you please. Your mother and I allow for it because you are so sensible and good. But my darling, you have not been raised around many children your age. You are not rich, but you are also not poor. This leaves you more vulnerable than you realise. With those blue eyes and that chestnut hair — why you'll have every young chap in London riding up here for my permission. I won't have it!"

My father's usual mild nature was replaced with irritation and perhaps, some fear. Quickly, I grabbed his hand again and brought it to my cheek.

"I'm sorry papa. I don't mean to upset you. I just want to see more of the world. That is all. I care nothing for chaps or gentlemen, as you call them."

Papa's voice was tender again, if not a little sad when he spoke to me.

"You say that now, my sweet Clara. The time will come though when you will replace your old papa with some bright-eyed lad. And I just know he won't be able to see straight the moment he lays eyes on you. It cannot be stopped. 'Mr. Edwards,' your mother often tells me in her most stern voice, which still sounds much like an angel, 'Clara Jane will be a woman soon and all the tears in the world will not stop it.' But I tell you, Clara, there will be tears."

I abandoned the topic then and there and spent time reading to both my mother and father out of my little poem book that evening to remind them that I wasn't yet grown.

*

As fate would have it, the tears came sooner than my father, mother, or I expected. After accepting my fate as an old spinster on the wild Yorkshire moors at the tender age of sixteen, I made peace by reading my favourite novels out there. One evening, the sun was not yet set, but in that magical fairy hour, right before twilight, I heard a soft whistling coming from the road below. I sat up, still hidden in the grass when a young man happened to be coming by. He was certainly a gentleman, with his black top hat and matching black coat. Though he looked friendly enough, as his whistling tune was pleasant, my instinct was to stay hidden until he passed.

I stayed very still, but the wind did not. As a wave rippled through the tall grass, my cover was revealed, and the handsome man looked over just in time to see me.

"Ho, hey! Little woman! What is such a small little fairy such as yourself doing hiding over there? I almost mistook you for a spectre. Look, the hair upon my arm is even in a fright."

I watched as he pulled back his sleeve to show he was being honest. His tone revealed that his scorn was in jest. I couldn't help but laugh. I stood up to greet him and then I laughed a little more.

"What is it?" he asked, now grinning.

"I am sorry sir. It's just - well, just now, I frightened you. It reminded me of my favourite novel. Though you didn't fall from your horse and you don't have a dog."

He gave me a knowing smile. "And you're no governess."

I bowed my head a little as my cheeks burned deeply. I didn't consider that he might have read the novel. "No sir."

"What is your name?"

"Clara. Clara Edwards."

"Well Miss Edwards, perhaps you wouldn't mind showing me to Dr Smith's home? Do you know it?"

"I do. And yes, I will show you."

The gentleman extended his arm to me and introduced himself as Mr Hugh Wilkes. He explained that he was visiting from London. Dr Smith was his cousin and had requested to see him for some time. Mr Wilkes thought it best to come during the summer, as our harsh northern winters were not for him. I could not fault him there and I told him so. I asked him why he didn't take a coach all the way over to Dr Smith's home.

"That would have been my preference. However, one of the carriage wheels broke and ended my journey prematurely. Fortunately, it was only a couple of miles from the house, and I preferred to walk rather than wait for it to be repaired. They'll bring my luggage later."

"What poor luck," I replied.

"Is it?"

"Well, sure."

"I think not," he laughed. "It seems to me that I have all the luck in the world. Here I have been dreading a trip this far north and all along, the jewel of England has been hiding in the heather." I blushed again and we parted with a friendly farewell.

I walked home with a fire in my chest. I thought of my papa and what he had said of those chaps in London. I doubted any there were as handsome as Mr Wilkes. As glad as I was to have met him, I doubted that I would see him again.

How wrong I was! Mr Wilkes came calling for me, along with Dr Smith to visit me, Mama, and Papa. Soon, he and I were good friends and called each other by our Christian names. When Papa would allow it, which was often enough thanks to Mama, Hugh and I would take walks along the moors, and sometimes we would visit some of the poorer households and deliver fresh eggs or flowers on Dr Smith's behalf.

Mr Wilkes was a true gentleman by birth and by nature. He was raised in London and had his home there. By midsummer, he told me that he had fallen in love with the moors, though he once thought it impossible. I showed him my drawings and even shared some of the poems I had written. He thought them lovely.

"The moors, they are a part of you."

"Yes - I suppose that is true," I replied. Hugh was leaning against an old tree as I sat in the grass, attempting to draw him.

"Have you been to London?" he asked. I looked up and he was smiling at me.

"No. I've always wanted to go, but papa won't allow it. Not yet, at least."

"Why is that?"

I laughed before replying. "He does not trust those 'London chaps'."

"He's right you know."

"About what?" I asked. Hugh walked over and took my hand, lifting me to meet him. Gently, he pulled me into his arms and kissed me. The heat moved from my chest to my ears as he pressed his soft lips upon mine. For a moment, the world around me ceased to exist and when it finally reappeared, Hugh proceeded to kiss my forehead head, and cheeks as he told me I was the most precious person he had ever met.

The day came when Hugh was to make his trip home to London. I cried myself to sleep the night before. I felt ridiculous. I knew he had a life to get back to in the city. The next morning Hugh was to come and say his farewell. When I made my way into the parlour that morning, my dear Hugh was sitting there with Papa. I fought hard to keep the tears away. They were unneeded. Papa excused himself and left us a moment.

"My darling girl, I find it impossible to return to London without you by my side. Sweet Clara, say you will marry me."

I wiped away the lone tear and looked at Hugh in

surprise. "But Papa..."

"No, darling, don't worry. He has agreed. I love you
with my heart and wish to take care of you so long as I live.
Please be my wife."

I did not hesitate again. I wrapped my arms around
Hugh and told him yes. Papa did break up our kiss but
married we were. After our small wedding, and after many
tears and kisses from mama and papa, Hugh and I were Mr
and Mrs Wilkes of London.

*

Then did I check the tears of useless passion -
Weaned my young soul from yearning after thine;
Sternly denied its burning wish to hasten
Down to that tomb already more than mine –
Emily Brontë

1862

Time hath not the power to remove thy memory from my
mind. My darling Hugh was six months gone from this world
when my mother came to London and brought me and my
young son home. I did my best to remain strong. I so wanted
to be like my mother. When Papa passed, she was stoic and
brave, comforting me through my grief. Now I could barely
make it through the day. Had I no child, I think I would have
met with the grave early.

Going home was the best thing for me; I had a routine.
Mama wouldn't let me sit still and suffer. Once the baby was
settled, I helped our old servant Aggie in the kitchen. My
tasks were small, but my hands were busy. I often picked
apples from the orchard or gathered flowers for the house. I
took the baby out for walks. Every day was a great effort, but
slowly, I was becoming more human again.

Hugh had been strong and vibrant, until one day, he
wasn't. The fever came on so suddenly that I could hardly
comprehend that he was lost to me. Ten years I had with my

love; we had built a life and a family together. Hugh was the darling of my heart, from the day I met him, we were inseparable.

Sometime in mid-spring, a few months after Mama brought me home, I woke up with a revitalized spirit. The days were growing warmer, and a small ray of hope glimmered somewhere deep in my sad soul. I had less difficulty with my mundane tasks and with the baby being exceedingly well, I decided to get some air.

I soon found myself out wandering the moors. It had been many years since I had walked upon the heather and lay beneath the tall grass. I gave no thought to which direction I went. I breathed in the fragrant cool air and just sauntered with one foot leading the other. For once, my mind was still. I recognised the feeling - it was peace. As soon as I gave it a name, it fled from me, leaving behind the grief and guilt that lay dormant in the soil. I dropped to my knees and wept. Every hidden feeling, I let surface. My chest was tight, my cheeks were wet, and my own voice was like a stranger's as the deep moaning echoed into the air.

After a while, when my tears were spent, I lay subdued in the grass with jots of purple heather all around me. I lay as still as a corpse as I watched the gentle wind make its way through the grassland and then through the melancholy leaves of the tree before me. I sat up, realising whose shadow I now lay under. It was the same spot where I had met my dear Hugh.

Tears fell down my cheeks - not the loud and painful ones I had shed a few moments before, but soft and knowing tears. It was as though he led me here himself, reminding me of our love. Though he was gone now, our love was not. I smiled to myself as I wiped away the wetness from my face.

"My darling love," I whispered, "thank you."

It was then I heard another person coming up the road. This time, it was my mother holding my darling son in her arms. My angel ran to me as Mama set him down and then she, too, took a seat in the grass next to me. We all sat in silence for a while, before she handed me a small book. I opened it to see that it was blank.

"Do you remember that small book of poems I gave you for your tenth birthday?"

"I do. Poems by Currer, Ellis, and Acton Bell." I stated. "You know, mama, they were all women. Currer wrote *Jane Eyre*."

"Your favourite novel."

"Yes." I smiled.

"Daughter?"

"Yes, Mama?"

"Perhaps, it is time you write." I took my mother's hand; it had aged over the years, but it was just as soft and gentle as ever before. I kissed it before responding. "Yes, I suppose you're right. My poems though - they will be different now." I felt the tears return.

"Oh yes, my love. You once wrote from a place of wonder. Now, you will write from experience. It is a gift bought at a great price."

Mama was right. Love is a great gift but to bear it, we all will pay with sorrow.

A Little While, A Little While

By Katrina Reilly

7.45 am

Judy unlocked her classroom door and switched on the light.
Before she had a chance to close the door behind her, Mrs
Metcalfe slipped in through the gap.

"Morning Judy! I'm glad you're in early. Can I ask you
a quick question about the phonics scheme?"

"Of course. Do you mind if I just take my coat off
first?" responded Judy, suiting action to words and shaking
the raindrops off her coat. As she did so Mrs Metcalfe settled
herself down in Judy's chair and put her coffee cup on Judy's
desk. Judy pulled off her winter boots and fumbled in her
rucksack for her indoor shoes, all the while watched by Mrs
Metcalfe who had a false, cheery, early-morning smile on her
face that did little to hide her customary irritation. Judy pulled
up one of the children's plastic chairs to sit on.

"How can I help?" she inquired.

"Would you mind just quickly going through the
phonics scheme with me? I'm teaching phonics period 2," Mrs
Metcalfe asked, her face beaming with the pretence of
friendliness.

"Weren't you in the training last night?" asked Judy, "I
spent an hour and a half going through the whole scheme in
quite a lot of detail." She had also spent a great deal of her
own time over the past few weeks preparing the training
materials - breaking the scheme down into a simple how-to
guide, complete with PowerPoint slides, internet links and
ready-made worksheets.

Mrs Metcalfe's smile wavered for a moment before she
determinedly forced it back onto her face with renewed
vigour.

"No, I missed the training, I'm afraid, could you go
through it with me now please?" She picked up her coffee cup

and took a sip, revealing a smudged ring of coffee left on Judy's desk. Judy looked at the clock and sighed.

"Okay, let me log on and I can send you the PowerPoint slides from last night."

Mrs Metcalfe's smile fractured, her face showing the impatience that she could no longer be bothered to mask.

"I don't really have time for slides and things. Could you just explain quickly what I need to do in the first lesson?" She put her coffee cup down on Judy's planning folder, leaving an imperfect dark circle of smeared coffee. Judy's eye twitched. She had come in early to get some worksheets printed out for her first two lessons. This was always the way at Lamb Hill School, it didn't matter how early she got in or how late she stayed, she never had a minute to herself.

She logged onto the computer, found her slides and carefully explained each one to Mrs Metcalfe (a pointless exercise that Mrs Metcalfe could have completed without Judy's assistance). After printing out the necessary worksheets for Mrs Metcalfe (again, a task that the older lady could easily have done for herself) Judy politely but firmly ejected Mrs Metcalfe from her chair and her classroom.

Just as Mrs Metcalfe left, Lucie, Judy's Teaching Assistant, arrived. Lucie was young and enthusiastic, a state that Judy vaguely recalled from her own youth, many hundreds of years ago. School years are like dog years, one year in school feels like seven years of normal human life. Lucie – bless her and preserve her – had brought Judy in a cup of tea. Judy thanked her profusely and gratefully took the warming cup. She then finally got the chance to open up her year 8 folder on the computer and look for her worksheets for the day's lessons.

"I didn't get a chance to tell you about what happened at hometime yesterday," said Lucie, taking off her coat. "There was a punch-up between Alfie and Ronnie; Ronnie bit his tongue and there was blood everywhere, all down his shirt and everything." Judy looked up from her computer.

"I didn't see an incident report about it," she said, "Who rang their parents?"

"Um, I don't think anyone did. I thought that was your job as form tutor?" said Lucie with a worried look.

"Well, yes," said Judy, a trifle impatiently, "But I couldn't ring them yesterday, as you only just told me about it just now."

"Yeah. Maybe you could ring them now?" suggested Lucie sheepishly.

Judy opened up her emails to see four emails from Ronnie's mum and one from Alfie's parents. Opening the last one, she could see that Ronnie's mum had cc'd in the Headteacher and the Chair of Governors. Judy took a deep breath. She looked over to the clock by her noticeboard.

8.15 am

Her eye wandered to the noticeboard where, next to her timetable and the class charter, she had pinned a postcard showing Emily Brontë in profile against a sea of purple heather. A beautifully calligraphed script read 'No coward soul is mine.' Judy shut her eyes and took another deep breath. *No coward soul is mine.* She opened her eyes, picked up the phone and called Ronnie's mum.

8.36 am

Judy hung up the phone and took a sip of her tea, which was now stone cold. She opened up the recording system on her computer to log the details of the phone call and to create an incident report about an incident that she hadn't witnessed and hadn't been informed of, but she was still, apparently, responsible for. The phone rang. It was her line manager informing her that they had a new pupil starting in her class this morning. The girl's parents had brought her in early and wanted to "briefly" meet with her form tutor before they left.

Judy opened the Year 8 folder on her desk and hastily printed off thirty-two copies of the first worksheet she saw.

Then she put a smile on her face, stopped being Judy and became Mrs O'Neill, the capable and responsible teacher. Fifty per cent of teaching is acting, putting on a performance. Smile, and stay calm. *No coward soul is mine*! Mrs O'Neill stepped out to meet her audience.

9 am

Most of the class had arrived and were taking off their wet coats and leaving them on books, folders, worksheets, and displays - basically anything made of paper that could be ruined by rainwater.

"Put your coats on your pegs please!" said Mrs O'Neill in a cheerful voice. A few pupils picked up their coats and put them on their pegs. "James, Bradley, Ellie – did you hear what I said? Coats on your pegs please!" James scowled at her as if she had asked him to poke himself in the eye with a sharpened stick rather than hang his coat on his peg. He threw his coat on the floor and kicked it.

"Mrs O'Neill! James just threw his coat on the floor AND he kicked it!" said Kayleigh. "Like this!" she added, showing an energetic kicking motion, in case Mrs O'Neill hadn't quite understood.

"Yes, Kayleigh, I saw..." began Mrs O'Neill, just as James directed his second kick in Kayleigh's direction. Mrs O'Neill stepped in front of Kayleigh and took James' kick full on the shin. She winced. *No coward soul is mine.* "Right, James, that's quite enough! Go outside and wait for me in the corridor."

"YOU'RE ALWAYS PICKING ON ME!" shouted James, "I WASN'T EVEN KICKING YOU, I WAS KICKING STUPID KAYLEIGH, IT'S YOUR OWN STUPID FAULT IF YOU GOT IN THE WAY!"

"Mrs O'Neill?" said Stanley, rummaging through the papers on Judy's desk. "We already did these worksheets last week."

12.30 pm

Judy had made it through Year 7 English (stressful), Year 8 Maths (unsuccessful), Break Duty (bedlam), Year 10 English (a total wash-out), and a truly horrific Year 9 Music lesson that they had all agreed they would never mention again.

12.31 pm

Judy got her first break of the day. She slipped into the ladies' toilets, entered a cubicle and locked the door. Another line of Emily Brontë's poetry entered her mind:

"A little while, a little while,
The weary task is put away." Emily had been a school teacher, Emily understood. "A little while, a little whi..."

"Mrs O'Neill? Are you in here?" The voice came through the door. For a fleeting moment, Judy considered keeping quiet and pretending she wasn't there. Responsible Mrs O'Neill overrode Judy's desire for a few moments of peace.

"Hang on a moment," she called back before reluctantly opening the door. It was Mrs Carlisle, the playground manager.

"Sorry to interrupt your break. Is Ronnie Simpson one of yours? He's just hit Alfie Greene round the head with a stick."

1.26 pm

Mrs O'Neill returned to her classroom from the student support unit where she had spent her lunch "break" helping Alfie and Ronnie work through their "friendship issues". Despite Ronnie ending the conversation by making some decidedly uncomplimentary comments about Alfie's mum, the student support team had decided that this was good progress as the boys were no longer physically assaulting each other, and they could therefore return to class for their afternoon lessons. This was even though Alfie had clearly indicated that he perceived the comments about his mum to be incendiary enough to require a resumption of hostilities at a future time, as yet unspecified.

Sitting at her desk Judy wondered whether she would have time to eat her hummus sandwich in the four minutes before she needed to go and collect her class from the playground, or whether she should just start writing up an incident report about the lunchtime fracas. Instead, she opened a tube of pringles and was just about to put one in her mouth when her class appeared at the door.

"Mrs O'Neill, Mrs Carlisle says that it's starting to rain and so we all need to come back to class," said Kayleigh, taking off her wet coat and placing it carefully on top of a pile of Maths work from the morning's lesson, whilst the rest of the class clambered in behind her, dropping damp scarves, gloves and woolly hats wherever they happened to fall.

Only one more lesson to go, Judy thought to herself, wearily, putting down the pringles.

2.15 pm

Period 6, the last lesson of the day was Judy's planning period. She sent her class off to their P.E. lesson with a hopeful smile on her face. She had forty-five minutes before the end-of-day registration. Forty-five minutes to herself.

"Where wilt thou go, my harassed heart?" she pondered to herself. Sadly, no escape to a Gondalian world within beckoned her. She had reports to write and tomorrow's lessons to plan, as well as marking to do. She might take five minutes out to eat her lunch first though. She opened her lunchbox and picked up her sandwich. The classroom door burst open.

"Mrs O'Neill! Mr Peterson says that we can't do P.E. on the field 'cause it's raining again!" said Ollie. Mr Peterson followed Ollie through the door.

"Sorry, Mrs O'Neill, do you mind if we use your classroom for P.E.?"

Mrs O'Neill sighed and reluctantly put her sandwich back in her lunchbox.

"No problem," she said, "I'll get out of your way."

2.20 pm

Judy put her head round the staffroom door and immediately decided against entering. The Head of Science appeared to be having a heated row with a menacing group of Geography teachers over who had jammed the photocopier. They were giving off Jets and Sharks vibes, and Judy sensed that things were about to get ugly. She quietly shut the door and sneaked off.

2.21 pm

Judy wandered along the corridor hoping to find an unoccupied classroom where she could settle down and get some work done. Each room that she passed was in use. A History lesson in here, a French lesson in there, a meeting with a parent in this one, a therapy session in that one. She tried the library but a lady with a Labrador informed her that the library was being used for canine therapy and no one who was not canine-trained would be allowed in for the rest of the day.

There was nowhere for her to go. She went upstairs to the admin offices, but they were also all occupied. She enquired at the door if there was a spare desk and computer that she could use for the next half hour. The admin staff laughed at the audacity of the question. A SPARE desk? Couldn't she see that they were stretched to capacity? They were having to share as it was!

> Why wilt thou go, my harassed heart,
> What thought, what scene invites thee now?
> What spot, or near or far,
> Has rest for thee, my weary brow?

Along the upper corridor, between the Food Tech room and the cleaners' cupboard, there was one door that was locked. Always locked. The stairs leading up to the attics were out of bounds to both staff and students. The attics were just storerooms for old school junk, but the staircase was unsafe. Only the caretaker had the key. Judy went down to his office. Barry, the caretaker, was on the phone. Judy smiled and pointed at the key cupboard and mouthed something unintelligible. Barry looked confused.

"Hang on a minute," he said. Judy just mouthed "thanks," gave Barry the thumbs up and palmed the key to the attic door.

2.35 pm

Judy checked that there was no one in the corridor before carefully unlocking the door and stepping through. She re-locked the door behind her with a scarcely audible click. The staircase was unlit, but the light filtering down from the attic window was enough to see by. She went slowly up the stairs, testing each tread before putting her weight on it. Halfway up a few steps were missing so she held on to the bannister and stretched her leg to the next unbroken tread, climbing slowly upwards.

At the top of the stairs was the main attic room. It was dusty and full of cobwebs and mouse droppings. There was little furniture other than a few broken chairs. Against the far wall were piles of old exam papers and leather-bound registers. There were also some very elderly-looking computer monitors and keyboards with letters missing. A few doorless doorways led off to smaller attic rooms, containing their own accumulations of dust, cobwebs and junk. Judy had been there before.

There was no sound except for the creaking floorboards as she stepped lightly across the room. She couldn't hear any voices, phones, slamming doors or running feet. Judy stepped delicately, deliberately over to the window, her shoes leaving prints in the dust. It was an old sash window and it opened with a gentle squeak. She looked out over the empty playground. The autumn treetops were a bright riot of colour, shiny with rainwater, and vibrant against the grey sky.

Judy breathed in deeply, the smell of rain on leaves evoking a long-forgotten memory of a childhood walk with her dad and her brother. They had been caught out in an unexpected shower. The dull grey-white sky had suddenly been hidden by a dark mass of heavy black cloud, bringing with it a sudden, drenching downpour. Judy had been frightened and cold and she had reached her arms up to her dad with a little bleat of terror. Laughing, he had swept her up in his arms and wrapped her up inside his coat; frightened and cold instantly became safe and warm in daddy's arms. The memory faded.

The attic had a musty, comforting smell of old books. Judy wiped the dust from a small area of the floor with her shoe. She lowered herself down and sat cross-legged by the window, slowly breathing in the cold air that drifted in. An occasional breeze lifted the dust off the floor and sent it across the room in small flurries before leaving it to settle back down again on the wooden floorboards.

Judy closed her eyes. She was on a clifftop, gazing down on a clear blue sea. Brightly coloured boats with white sails scuttered by. The sea glittered, sparkled, and danced in the sunlight. She clamoured down some wooden steps to a rocky seashore, the rough wood warm against the soles of her bare feet. A lighthouse striped red and white, like a helter-skelter ride at the fairground, stood sentinel just out from the coast, lending the scene a festive air. Seaweed-covered boulders dotted the beach, hollows of water between them left behind by the tide.

Her sun-browned feet found footholds on the slippery rocks as she scrambled across, peering into rockpools where tiny fish darted, their bodies flashing, reflecting the sunlight. Crabs peeped out from the shadows. Limpets clung to the rock. Unhurried, Judy stepped into the water. The soft squelch of sand felt heavenly between her toes, the water warm and inviting. She breathed. She breathed. The sun on her face, the sea lapping at her ankles. She reached up her arms and stretched to the sky.

Peace. Her shoulders relaxed. Her jaw un-clenched. Her breathing slowed. A brief moment of solace for her soul. A brief moment. Brief. Too brief. She opened her eyes. Emily knew.

> Could I have lingered but an hour,
> It well had paid a week of toil...
> Even as I stood with raptured eye,
> Absorbed in bliss so deep and dear,
> My hour of rest had fleeted by,
> And back came labour, bondage, care.

Emily had been a school teacher, Emily understood. Judy stood up, shut the window, went down the stairs, and locked the door. Mrs O'Neill went back to her classroom.

2.59 pm

She opened the classroom door.

"Thank you, Mr Peterson," said Mrs O'Neill, "I'm back for afternoon registration." Mr Peterson, looking a damn sight more frazzled than he had forty-five minutes ago, nodded a curt goodbye. A chorus of voices rose up to greet her, issuing from a small, winsome, tyrant army with arms upstretched.

"Mrs O'Neill, I can't find my water bottle!"

"Mrs O'Neill, my jumper is inside out!"

"Mrs O'Neill, I need the toilet!"

"Mrs O'Neill, I've drawn a picture of you," said Stanley. She looked at the picture. A glorious medley of primary colours showed a smiling teacher surrounded by happy, smiling children. She smiled.

"Thank you, Stanley," she said.

The Dancing Master

By Emmeline Burdett

The British Library had almost become Dora Kempe's' second home. It was not only the allure of the gift shop and the tempting array of treats available in its cafés (although it would be foolish to deny that these *were* part of its charm) but the fact that its Reading Rooms offered a space in which Dora could think. Today, however, Dora had - rather reluctantly, it has to be said - decided to forgo her customary visit to the café in preference for going straight to the Rare Books and Music Reading Room. Once in her seat, she carefully opened the package that the librarian had given her, and found that it contained a letter, which read as follows.

Halifax

3rd September 1855

My dear Sir

A young relative of mine drew my attention to your recent advertisement in the London Times, in which you sought reminiscences of the late Currer Bell.

I was privileged to attend Roe Head School at the same time as Miss Brontë (as she then was) and I well remember that she used to take delight in 'entertaining' us with ghost stories, which were often of such a character that slumber deserted us for some time afterwards.

One of the tales she told us concerned the lady with rustling skirts who, it was said, haunted parts of the house. I trust that my recollection of the tale may prove a useful addition to your collection of reminiscences.

I arrived at Roe Head School a little before Miss Brontë, towards the end of the year 1830. The weather was chill and damp, and I arrived feeling stiff and cold, having sat almost motionless in my aunt's carriage for some hours. Bodily discomfort notwithstanding, however, I was eager to embark upon this new stage of my life and excited to meet my new companions.

My parents had both died in India, and, after my return to England, the maiden aunts who had (somewhat against their better judgement, I fear) agreed to take me in were only too glad to send me away to the new school which had been opened by their old friend Miss Margaret Wooler and some of her sisters.

By this time, I had grown well accustomed to adapting to whatever new situation I happened to find myself in, and it did not take me long to feel that Roe Head might indeed grow to be a safe haven in what had recently been a rather tumultuous life. I had managed to find some friends amongst the other girls, and I loved the house — which was about one hundred years old — and its surroundings.

Back in the British Library Reading Room, Dora tutted rather impatiently. The as-yet-unnamed writer of the letter had said that she had arrived at Roe Head shortly before Charlotte, but Charlotte herself – and the promised ghost story – had yet to make an appearance. Dora read on.

My first glimpse of Miss Brontë was not very promising, and yet, it did arouse my compassion. She arrived on a covered cart, one cold January day, and she looked rather like a little old woman. Miss Brontë had evidently been somewhat loth to leave her friends, for, at the commencement of her time with us, she looked extremely miserable. The house, though, soon worked its magic upon her, as it had upon me.

At night, when we girls were all in bed, she fell into the habit of telling us stories. This is one that I remember with particular clarity.

The house was built one hundred years ago as a private dwelling .It was built for a man named Captain Thomas Lovell, and for his new wife Cassandra. Captain Lovell had dark hair and eyes, and an imperious, forbidding manner. Cassandra was a beauty, and it was said that she could have married any man she chose. She had long golden ringlets, which she wore in the very latest style. Her graceful neck and her fingers glittered with jewels, and her dresses —

"Might benefit from a little less description," muttered Dora. Aware that she would probably be asked to leave the Reading Room if she continued her commentary on what she was reading, she resolved to continue her task in silence.

Captain Lovell was acutely aware that he was not an attractive man, and for this reason he was always afraid that his new wife would tire of him and seek happiness in the arms of another. The fact that they had married for love, and that Cassandra showed absolutely no inclination to stray, did nothing to calm his fears.

Cassandra was, in fact, fully occupied with visiting her husband's tenants. She had told Captain Lovell that she had no wish to be a mere decoration — someone who possessed a few impressive 'accomplishments' but was of no real use to anyone else. She saw that her husband's tenants were poor and often ill, and she relished the opportunity to make their lives a little easier.

So involved was she in her task that her husband's fears gave way to embarrassment over the amount of time she devoted to it. He attempted to explain to her that it was not seemly for a lady of her rank to associate quite so persistently with such low-born and ignorant persons, but Cassandra merely laughed.

'What would you have me do?' she asked. 'Your tenants need me. I enjoy their company, and YOU do nothing to improve their lives. If you would only accompany me on my visits, you would see how small and dark their cottages are. They become smoky whenever a fire is lit, and at such times it really becomes very difficult indeed to breathe.'

'But they do not mind that!' retorted her husband. 'It is only you who does. You are accustomed to large, well-ventilated rooms. If you spent as much time here as you do going a-visiting, you would be more accustomed to them still. I must be more careful with you'.

'I am quite robust,' said Cassandra. 'You need not fear that I will suffer any lasting harm from visiting your tenants, and I am really rather annoyed that you should be more concerned about the sufferings that you imagine I experience rather than those that your tenants actually experience'.

'The cottages have chimneys!' said Captain Lovell. 'It is rather hard to see how lighting a fire would make them fill with smoke. I am merely concerned that being out of doors in all kinds of weather will make you ill, and I have already explained that you are affected by smoky cottages only because you are not accustomed to them. I am also a person of no little importance in this part of the world, and my wife should not demean herself and forget her station by associating with her inferiors.'

Cassandra's spirit was one of the things that had originally attracted her husband, but now that they were married, it was also proving to be the thing that risked making her too difficult to control. He was determined to make her more like the wife of a landed gentleman and began to turn his mind to the question of how it might be done.

The following day was grey and rainy, and Cassandra stared disconsolately out of the breakfast-room window.

'Come and eat something!' implored her husband. 'Cook has really excelled herself this morning. Imagine how she would feel if her efforts went unappreciated.

Cassandra turned away from the window, and her eyes flashed. 'I suppose you wish me to appease Cook and simply forget about the cottagers?'

'Well, they will hardly be suffering from the rain — they work inside their cottages.''

'Did you not even know that their cottages are in a poor state of repair and let the rain in? Why must you be so contemptuous of the comfort of your fellow creatures? These are your tenants, and surely you realise that they are your responsibility!'.

Captain Lovell sighed and went back to his newspaper. His eye was caught by an advertisement placed by a dancing master who was obviously on the hunt for new pupils. He would not previously have thought of willingly introducing his wife to another man, but he imagined with pleasure someone foppish and rather effeminate whom the fiery Cassandra could not possibly consider attractive.

He resolved to write to the dancing master and explain that he wished to engage him for his wife, who was somewhat deprived of occupation and stimulating company. He would not, of course, tell the dancing master that his aim in engaging him was principally to deprive Cassandra of the occupation she already had.

Some ten days later, Cassandra arrived home from a visit to her husband's tenants to find that her husband himself was waiting for her. By his side was an unfamiliar gentleman with a long grey wig and a blue frock coat. Captain Lovell took Cassandra's arm and pulled her towards him.

'My treasure, I was just explaining to Mr Burney that you have been rather lonely since coming to live here with me. If you were a more proficient dancer, it would be easier for me to take you out to other great houses. I am sorry to say — 'He turned to Mr Burney. 'I am sorry to say that my dear Cassandra has been obliged to visit my tenants for want of proper society. I am sure you will agree that such associations are wholly unsuitable for a lady of her rank. I am a busy man and cannot give her all the attention she requires.'

Cassandra felt that she could not let this false description of her pass entirely unchallenged. She retorted rather indignantly that she derived much from visiting the tenants, that she enjoyed their company, that she was not at all lonely and certainly did not require constant attention. Furthermore, she had very little interest in dancing.

Captain Lovell smiled indulgently. 'I applaud your bravery, my dear, but do think of your position as my wife. How can I go into society alone? People will wonder why you do not accompany me.'

Cassandra privately wondered where her husband's newly acquired desire to go out into society had come from. One thing that had drawn them together had been their mutual dislike of spending hour after hour in the company of people for whom the saying 'The Devil makes work for idle hands' could quite conceivably have been invented.

'Besides, my dear,' continued Captain Lovell, 'Mr Burney has travelled all the way from London to help us. Surely you would not be so cruel as to send him all the way back again?'

Rather against Cassandra's better judgment – although it did not seem to matter a great deal what she felt – it was arranged that Mr Burney would come to the house every day. He would attempt to transform Cassandra into the decoration she had never wanted to be. Captain Lovell rejoiced inwardly at this development and hoped that his wife would prove to be an industrious, but not particularly gifted, pupil.

His joy soon turned to suspicion, though. He had purchased a piano for his wife's special use, but though he listened closely, he seldom heard its strains and wondered how it was possible to learn dancing with so little in the way of musical accompaniment. Perhaps his wife was making very slow progress indeed.

Cassandra was surprised and rather pleased to discover that Mr Burney seemed strangely unwilling to teach her the fundamentals of dance. He seemed to prefer to converse, showing an interest in her that her husband had not done since the earliest days of their courtship. That is to say, he seemed to prefer that she should converse: whilst he was eager to learn every detail of her life, he was not disposed to discuss his origins or opinions.

'Are you really a dancing master?' asked Cassandra one morning. 'You have not taught me to dance a step, and my husband is growing rather suspicious. I have told you that he does not have a trusting nature, and he perceives that I make no progress. I fear he no longer believes my claims of lack of talent and lack of interest.

'Well, then', replied Mr Burney, 'Perhaps we ought to try harder to convince him of our commitment to the task before us'.

He sat down at the piano and began to play an unexpectedly lively gavotte. Cassandra tried her best to keep up and gambolled a few hastily invented steps which, she hoped, kept reasonable time with the music. When she was thoroughly exhausted, she sat down beside him for a rest. This proved to be something of a mistake, as such close proximity made their mutual attraction much harder to ignore.

Mr Burney took a deep breath and began to speak. 'As you correctly perceive, I am not a dancing master. Had I been, then I flatter myself that you would have made some progress, however slight. Indeed, my name is not even Mr Burney'.'

Cassandra was aware that this revelation should have made her feel disappointed, even betrayed. She tried to play the role which she assumed was expected of her. She rose to her feet.

'Mr — whoever you are! Am I to understand that you have been accepting my husband's money under false pretences? I ought to have you dismissed from the house, never to return!'

He looked crestfallen. 'If such is to be my fate, then I beg of you to act quickly. Do not prolong my agony.' Cassandra looked at him, surprised by the apparent violence of his passion. She was determined that she would give him no encouragement.

'Whatever can you mean? My husband engaged you to teach me to dance! He apparently wants to go out into society and feels he cannot do it with a woman who wants to discuss serious subjects.'

The former dancing master sighed heavily. Cassandra decided that she would take pity on him. She asked him why he had felt it necessary to assume another identity. He thought for a moment and then spoke.

'My true name is James Francis. My family has never been rich but has always had pretensions of being so. Since my earliest infancy, it has been understood that I would make what my parents believed to be an advantageous match, to the daughter of an acquaintance of my father's – the heiress to a large fortune. I was introduced to her for the first time some months ago, and I knew at once that she was the last woman that I could ever marry. Our tastes, our thoughts - all were completely at odds.

'I attempted to explain to my father that our union would be impossible, but he was adamant. He saw her fortune as his entry into society, and my happiness was of no consequence to him. I resolved then that I must abandon my life, and so James Francis, a sacrificial lamb, became Peter Burney, a dancing master.' He laughed rather mirthlessly.

'What will you do?', asked Cassandra. 'Are you going to learn how to teach dancing?'.

'Yes, why not? As you see, I can already play the piano'.

'But you will be lonely. You may not have wanted to marry your intended bride, but that does not mean that you wish to spend your life alone.'

'I was rather hoping that you might wish to spend it

with me'.

As proposals went, Mr Burney's — or rather, Mr Francis' — left something to be desired. Nevertheless, Cassandra needed little encouragement to respond to it. She took his hand.

'Come back at midnight. My husband retires early, and he will be sound asleep by then. We can make our escape.'

At midnight Mr Francis crept back towards the house as he had been instructed. He knew instinctively that, just as with his father, there was no point attempting to explain to Captain Lovell that he and his wife would only ever succeed in making one another miserable. He was so immersed in his thoughts that he did not hear a step behind him. Someone caught hold of his arm.

'Well, well,' whispered Captain Lovell. 'It's a little late for a dancing lesson, is it not? I do admire your dedication to your chosen profession.'

Mr Francis opened his mouth to speak, but Captain Lovell tightened his grip upon his arm and forced him towards the open front door. They heard light footsteps upon the stairs.

'Were you going somewhere?' enquired Captain Lovell. 'I'm afraid to say that your travelling companion is indisposed'. He drew his sword across Mr Francis' throat.

Cassandra looked at her husband in horror, as he wiped his sword clean and replaced it in its scabbard. He hauled his wife back up the stairs and locked her in an attic room on the third floor. '

'What happened next?' we all asked.

'What could happen next?' asked Miss Brontë. 'Captain Lovell was well-connected. He had Francis's body buried in the *grounds and managed to suppress the inevitable questions regarding his sudden disappearance. He was soon forgotten.'*

'But what happened to Cassandra?'

'She forgot him too, although she did not intend to. After witnessing his violent death, she began to go mad. Her husband kept her locked up in the attic room and fed her just enough to keep her alive. Even so, she died about five years later. But she is still looking for Francis, and still, perhaps, hoping to run away with him.'

I hope that this eerie tale will enhance your collection of reminiscences of the unfortunate Currer Bell.

I have the honour to be, Sir, very truly yours,
Mrs Ellen De Vere.

Dora replaced the letter in its box and returned it to the librarian. She left the Reading Room in silence, but she decided not to visit the café.

A World of Our Own

By Nicola Friar

In the summer of 2016, I was ensconced within the walls of the Brontë Parsonage Museum's library. Surrounded by fragile tomes and manuscripts, I was there to research Charlotte's early works of fiction for my dissertation. Others in my classes at university trod more obvious tracks - the published works of often rich and privileged established authors. The ones with an education and the finest material goods in life. I had no interest in those who'd had access to the fanciest college rooms, the grand ancestral homes, and the overflowing vaults in the banks. I cast aside those authors born into the upper echelons did not I wanted to know more about the women who, in order to write, had created entire worlds to inhabit and in doing so had inspired generations of women in so many ways.

The summer day was sultry but the library was cool and the atmosphere tranquil. In my hands, I held a tiny book created by Charlotte Brontë and her siblings almost two centuries earlier. In my hands, I held an entire world. I tenderly turned the delicate pages, in awe at the determination of the sisters (and Branwell) to do what they wanted to do - write. However, unlike their brother, Charlotte, Emily, and Anne had continued to build their own ancestral homes in their adult life and populated them with females looking for independence, freedom, and a place to call their own. Glass Town, Angria, and Gondal had walked so that Thornfield, Wuthering Heights, and Wildfell Hall could soar.

As I gazed at the book I wondered how they would have felt at seeing their space invaded so freely and so casually by hands and eyes such as my own. Would they be pleased or sad? Or perhaps even angry. Remembering the anecdotes about Charlotte's discovery of Emily's poems, I thought she would have seen it as a gross violation of her privacy, and possibly even her identity. Anne may have had milder feelings; perhaps blushing but acknowledging the words and the freedom they offered her.

And Charlotte? What would she think? She preserved and protected the manuscripts for the remainder of her life. Maybe they were a link to the freedom she craved in adulthood. Uncensored, unrestricted, and undisturbed in their hiding place. What would she think of me?

My mind wandered as I gazed out of the window. My eye found the outline of St. Michael's church just a stone's throw from where I sat. My fingers found the pencil as my imagination travelled to where most of the Brontë family were buried - in the vault beneath the floor. Again, I wondered what Charlotte would think and wrote what I hoped she would.

*

I rose from my resting place and glided through the building in search of an exit. Something had disturbed me. I could not get my bearings. I knew not where I was. I last closed my eyes at home. That place was not home. I longed for air, I longed for space, and I longed for freedom. I could not breathe.

The smell of pew wood and leather told me it was a church that I wandered through. I could see only the silhouettes of the objects surrounding me. Familiar to me by day, they became monstrous in the eerie half-light. On locating a door, I perceived the way was barred to me, but I quickly found that the wood and metal could not hold me.

The outside world that greeted me was silent and still. All was dark, the sky was velvety black, and the stars were shining clear and cold above. The night wind was crisp and refreshing. The world was alive. Still, I could not breathe.

I glanced up at the building I had just left. As I did so, I could see it was a new building. Different in size and shape, it loomed above me threateningly. It was not my papa's church. It was not my church.

I shook off my sense of disorientation and grounded myself. I looked around me. The church had tricked me, but I knew where I was. The balmy Haworth night embraced me. But was it still my Haworth?

Nearby the houses still stood along the lane overlooking the graveyard. Their shadows stretched across to meet me as I stood at the entrance to the church. I could sense the souls within as their inhabitants slumbered temporarily. I turned away towards the resting place of those who slumbered permanently in the graveyard. There the shadows danced and played games with the moonlight.

How can a graveyard feel so alive? I pondered this as I scrambled around the tombs and headstones in front of the church. I could see the outline of another building in the near distance. I was desperate to reach it. The wind shook the leaves on the trees, and they whispered to me, urging me onwards, urging me home.

As I reached the final row of graves, I tried unsuccessfully to enter the parsonage garden via the kissing gate. I was tantalisingly close, but on reaching the spot I found a solid wall in its place. The way was barred to me. I could not overcome the obstacle in my path. It was not my graveyard.

I stumbled back over the headstones and returned to the lane. I glided over the cobbles past the houses until I reached the schoolroom. It was the place where I had toiled and attempted to impart my knowledge to the local children. It was a place I had earned my living. My papa had taught me to be useful to society. I taught others from humble backgrounds how to do the same. But I was a woman who wanted to write. What use was that to anybody else? What use was it to me?

I had no wish to teach. The schoolroom was just another instrument of restraint. The sight of it suffocated me. Teaching had been a way to earn a living, but it was never my life. I was a cog that had perpetuated the belief that literature was not the business of a woman's life. I did not wish to dwell on my time trapped between those four walls. It was time to close the door.

I heard a creaking sound and glanced up to see a sign swing eerily at the side of the parsonage. I moved closer and squinted up at it. By the yellow light of the crescent moon, I made out the silhouette of a woman sitting at a writing desk. I smiled at it, thinking of my dear sisters.

A tall and unfamiliar gate threatened to bar my way. There were so many obstacles. I reached out, and the gate swung open noiselessly at my touch. I found myself in the parsonage garden. The moonlight guided me as I studied my surroundings. The lawn was pristine, and the flower beds were elegant. It was not my garden.

I turned towards the building I had been so desperate to reach. It had grown in size and had extra rooms. Whose rooms were they? Did they belong to the woman on the sign? How glorious it must be to have a home of one's own.

No light was visible in the tall windows, but the front door was wide open to admit the still night air and anybody who cared to enter. Did I dare? The path was in no way barred, but I hovered uncertainly on the threshold, wondering what changes I would find inside and whether I wanted to see them.

I stepped back. I found that I lacked the courage to enter. It was not my parsonage. I had no business there. I took a final look up at the building and murmured a quiet goodbye. But before I turned away, a light blazed above me. It seemed to be coming from the room at the top of the staircase, but I knew its origins were in Glass Town, in Angria, and in Gondal. It was a beacon that called me home.

Without further thought, I entered through the front door and walked across the dark hallway. I could see a soft glow on the staircase as I ascended it. I paused at the grandfather clock and pictured my papa winding it up each night on his way to his bedroom. I glanced out of the window that overlooked the fields at the back of the parsonage. All was dark within and without. I did not linger. The light was calling me.

I reached the nursery, where the door stood open in welcome. The golden light emitting from it invited me in, and I stepped over the threshold into the past. In my mind's eye, I saw pirates, beautiful ladies, dashing heroes, and noble poets. There were explorers, kings, queens, ladies, and lords. I saw castles and palaces, great oceans full of ships and fairies flitting around like fireflies.

It was over in seconds, and I stood alone in the room. Yet the light did not extinguish. I could see a small bed, scribbles on the wall, a group of toy soldiers, and, best of all, I could feel the presence of my siblings. We had been budding writers and Chief Genii in that room. It had been *our* room.

I left the door open as I descended the staircase. I did not bother with any of the rooms I passed. They were not mine. I had but one destination in mind. I could see the light shining from around the closed doorway as I approached the old parlour leading off the hallway. I entered the shabby but neat little parlour leading off the hallway and my heart soared.

I saw the cheerful old fireplace and felt its warmth. I could taste hot tea and Tabby's crumbly muffins. I could feel the quill in my fingers and in my mind's eye I watched as the ink traced out the words that were always scrambling for release from my imagination. I could hear the sounds of my dear sisters' footsteps as they paced around the table where I sat with my writing.

That room was ours. The three of us would often walk, talk, and write whenever the mood was upon us. Sometimes we would stop to drink tea, eat cake, and enjoy each other's company. After a short break, we would begin again. Rejuvenated after the refreshments, stories and secrets would erupt from our quills in that ordinary little room.

We would hide away from the world. It may have been

our room and writing, but it was also our secret. It had to be. We were three sisters, mere women who should have been earning a living using the skills and knowledge our papa had endeavoured to have instilled into us.

The world was not ours; it did not understand. It did not care. We wanted to write, and we needed space in which to do this. It would never be freely given, and so it was stolen and secreted away. Just like in our faraway childhood years. However, there were differences that divided us.

Emily wished only to create and to write. That was where she found her place, her peace, and her freedom. She cared not for the prying eyes of others and the judgement she knew she would face from outsiders. She was a writer at heart she knew no greater pleasure. She did not appreciate my own prying eyes greedily devouring her work, her heart, and her soul. For Emily, my interest, and that of the world, was a gross intrusion into the life she lived independently of those around her. Her mind and her imagination were her own safe space. Emily's room was her mind.

Anne's devotion to our joint quest to see our work in print may seem strange to some. To those who did not know her, Anne was quiet and gentle. To us, she may have been a peacemaker and pacifier - she could smooth ruffled feathers and bruised pride better than anyone - but Anne was no wallflower. She had the courage to shine a light on the harsh brutality of reality for women of all classes and backgrounds. Anne's writing had a purpose, and she had a message.

What did I desire? I wrote because I could not help it. I may not have been a born author but I was born a writer. I had stories spilling out of me - ones not always suitable for a child, a young lady, or a grown woman - but out they came, flowing from my mind and onto whatever scraps of paper I could get my hands on. It had been a thrill when my words first appeared in print. It had been a disappointment when nobody read them. Like a tree in the woods falling when nobody is around, is a writer without readers an author? No.

And that is why I wrote. That is why I kept the tiny books - the child in me wanted to be an author. I wanted to ensure the child's voice would be heard. I wanted to ensure that the child's words were read.

I sat at the parlour table until the stars faded and sunlight began to sneak into the room. I heard noises; the sounds of footsteps and voices met my ear. I froze in a blind panic. This was not my home. Whose property was I trespassing on? It was someone with similar tastes to my own. Looking around the room in daylight I saw a set up that was remarkably familiar to me. It looked as though my sisters would join me at any moment. A creak outside the door made me glance around in hope but nobody appeared.

I could still hear voices and life all around me. It was as if the parsonage was waking up. Mustering my courage, I rose and walked softly out of the room. I was amazed to find the hallway just as I remembered it; the flagged stone floor could have just been scrubbed by Martha.

The kitchen door was ajar. Emily had enjoyed spending time in there by the fire with Keeper or helping with the baking, but it was not a room I had ever particularly enjoyed spending time in. It was Tabby's room and a place where she found some element of freedom as she cleaned, baked, chopped, and told stories that fed our imaginations as children. These tales found their way into our tiny books and helped to build our literary palaces, structures that were so much more than mere castles in the sky.

An overwhelming buzz of noise and activity met my ears from just outside the kitchen. I looked for an escape, a room in which to hide. I could not return from whence I had come for the voices were coming from the hallway. I caught sight of an unfamiliar door and grasped the knob, hoping to find myself in the field at the back of the parsonage. But times had changed, and time had changed the house; it was locked, and I was trapped.

This was not my home. I was an intruder waiting to be

caught. I knew nothing of those who inhabited the parsonage. And then I remembered that this was not my home. If I could only gain access to the extra rooms in the building then perhaps I could find freedom. At the back of the kitchen was another door. I grabbed the handle and found myself in a room full of books. It looked like a library. Oh, to have a library like this and the freedom to sit and read from dawn until dusk!

I wandered around the room, running my fingers along the spines of the volumes. I recognised many, including some of my own. There were too many volumes of *Jane Eyre* to count as well as the other novels penned by myself and my sisters. I heard a light scratching noise and was surprised to see a young woman sitting at a table in the centre of the room. Her long dark hair fell over her eyes as she leaned forward, squinting at something she held in her hands.

Intrigued, I moved closer. With astonishment I watched as she tried to decipher the text in the pages of the tiny book she held. More of our precious books were scattered across the table. I should have been concerned about what the world would think of us, about Emily's feelings of violation, and about Anne's blushes. But instead I rejoiced. The child writer was an author at last.

I watched as the woman tenderly placed the book on the wooden surface and gazed out the window. Seconds later she picked up her pencil and began to write, the words flowing fast. I smiled as I watched. A burden I had not realised I was carrying was lifted. I had preserved those books all my life and now a tear rolled down my cheek as I realised that others had safeguarded them after my death.

Any step on the road to freedom is important, no matter how seemingly small or insignificant. This woman, obviously part of a very different society to my own, was a part of our world. I looked out the window at the sign swinging in the breeze and read the words "Brontë Parsonage Museum."

Peeking over the woman's shoulder before returning to the church, I saw what she was writing -

Glass Town, Angria, and Gondal had walked so that Thornfield, Wuthering Heights, and Wildfell Hall could soar.

Non-Fiction

The Second Mrs Fred & the Johnson Women. Part I.

By Maria Johnson

"Time to pick up the boys."

Fred stole a glance at his wife as he prepared to carefully turn right onto Driftway Road. Thelma smiled at him and was relieved to see that the pavement was dry and that some sand remained from the most recent snowfall. A fairly steep and somewhat curvy road, it could be a challenge to navigate in the dead of winter, but thus far they had never failed to make it all the way to the top of the hill to their home. And never before had they had to make the journey with such a delicate - cargo their newborn daughter.

Trusting, as always, in her husband's ability to deal with wintry weather, Thelma was nonetheless a little anxious as the gathering clouds began to obscure whatever sunlight remained that afternoon. As the sunlight began to fade, the leafless trees and snow-covered ground on either side of the road created an almost eerie stillness, interrupted only by the whimpering and gurgling of the newborn.

As the road began to curve to the left, they pulled into the driveway of the house on the right. It was a boxy two-family home, with concrete steps leading to the second-floor terrace, over which a striped awning provided protection from the elements. Next to the garage door was an entrance to the larger home on the first floor in which lived Thelma's brother and his family; on the upper floor lived her parents.

Upon seeing the car pull into the driveway, doors opened, both up and down. From upstairs, Thelma's parents slowly made their way down the steps, bundled up against the January cold and stepping cautiously, wary of slipping on any unseen ice. Antonio was a solidly built man of average height, and his thick, wavy grey hair was brushed back from his forehead. Said forehead gave way to smiling, twinkling blue eyes that gave the impression of a man who was satisfied with his life, and, in case he wasn't, it didn't matter because he knew things - and he knew people.

Eva was a large woman, perhaps a bit above average height, but definitely a long way above average weight, tipping the scales not too far south of four hundred pounds - a size not as common in the 1950s as it may be today. Her thick, dark brown hair had barely a hint of grey, despite being in her mid-fifties, and she wore it pulled back in her customary bun. Her coal-dark eyes dominated a face which, unlike her husband's, was rarely seen to be smiling. This did not necessarily mean that she was unhappy, but her expression was nearly always grim. Perhaps this was a result of the fact that only two of her children, Freddy and Thelma, had survived infancy. Perhaps it was because her husband had often disappeared for days and weeks on end - presumably to visit his rumoured other family in a more southern state.

However, on this brisk day, a smile lit her face as she came partway down the stairs, handkerchief in hand, bundled up against the cold. As Thelma got out of the car to bring the baby over to meet her grandparents, Eva waved her off.

"I have a terrible cold and don't want the baby to catch it. I will hold little Maria plenty once I get over this cold." Antonio had no such qualms and came over right away to admire this new addition to his roster of grandchildren. As he did so, said grandchildren began to stream out of the door on the first floor, followed by his daughter-in-law Margie. Aunt Margie and Uncle Freddy had four daughters at that time, but would also be adding to their brood later in the year.

As the two families lived so close - on the same hill, but a half-mile apart - there was much to-ing and fro-ing and back-ing and forth-ing between the two families, and the two sets of cousins were almost always together.

"Come on, boys," said Fred to his two sons. "We've got to get your little sister home before it gets too much colder." The two boys took leave of their grandparents, aunt, and cousins, and scrambled into the car. The newly-expanded family continued its journey up the hill, eventually turning left onto a private road, and up a last, steep hill.

There were but four houses on this last hill, and theirs was the very last one, surrounded on three sides by the silent woods of winter. The two houses nearest theirs were not occupied at this time. The owners of these houses were two brothers who, like Fred, were Swedish immigrants. Despite being accustomed to harsher winter weather than is typical in Connecticut, both of these families would usually spend most of the winter months in New York City where they were employed, as was Fred.

Fred and Thelma (a native New Yorker) had also had an apartment in New York and would come to Connecticut in the warmer months. But both of them wanted to raise their children in a more rural setting and had thus given up their apartment to stay permanently in their holiday home shortly before their baby girl arrived. It is common in Sweden for folks to have a weekend home, even if they lived in a small town, and Fred, along with his friends Gus and Ted, had decided to continue that tradition in their new country.

They jointly purchased a parcel of land, not too far from the commuter train to New York, which they subdivided and distributed between them by drawing straws. Their weekend homes were humble at first (Fred's had only recently been updated to include an indoor bathroom) and built by their own hands. But they provided a peaceful escape from the bustle of the city.

Once home, Fred took the boys in hand so that Thelma could settle the baby in. As she lay her new daughter into the bassinette near their bed, she could not help thinking about what her own mother must have felt when she had brought little Thelma home from the hospital in 1925. Eva's and Antonio's other children had all been born at home, and only Freddy had made it past infancy. But by the time she was born, he was of school age, healthy and thriving, a real bruiser!

It had been seven years since Tony's birth and, content as they were with their family, Thelma and Fred often wondered if they would ever add to its number. Now, after all that time, she stood in their bedroom looking down at her new baby girl, Maria, who was named for her Swedish grandmother. She smiled. She thought she knew how her mother must have felt. And she was very happy, indeed.

Thelma stood and looked around as little Maria drifted off to sleep. There was the same pale green floral wallpaper as before, the same dark chest of drawers and bureau, the same Venetian blinds on the window - but it felt different somehow. She had always loved babies and young children and always enjoyed being around them, and she had never lacked for their company. She became an aunt at sixteen, and when she married Fred she had acquired a three-year-old stepson in Paul, whose mother had tragically died within days of his birth. Within a year of their marriage, Thelma was a mother herself having given birth to Tony, named in honour of her father.

She sat down on the bed, with its light brown bedspread covered with large chenille spots of a darker brown, looking like so many cookies on a giant baking sheet. She thought again of her mother. Her parents' marriage had not been the best, but for all that her father might come and go, her mother was always there - usually in the kitchen - full of wisdom and old wives' tales.

*

After school, Thelma climbed the stairs to their apartment in the Bronx, and before even opening the door, she could smell the tantalizing aroma of good food to come.

"What are we having tonight?" she asked as she kissed her mother.

"Meat sauce," Eva answered, wiping the sweat from her face with a corner of her apron. "You are just in time - I still need to add the tomatoes, then leave it to simmer for a while. Next -"

"Not now," Thelma interrupted her. "A couple of friends are coming over to study, and I want to change my clothes before they get here."

"Now, Thelma," this was a conversation they had had many times before, "how are you going to learn how to cook if you don't watch what I do? You need to learn how to make your own pasta and sausages and sauces. The way to a man's heart is through his stomach, you know, and how are you going to be able to cook anything good for your future husband if you don't learn now?"

"Yeah, yeah, yeah, Ma," she answered, it was all she could do to keep from rolling her eyes. "I could never be as good a cook as you, anyway. And, besides, I'm not in a big rush to get married. I'm having too much fun!" Eva turned back to the stove, adding the chopped tomatoes with several quick movements of her wooden spoon. "In fact," Thelma continued, "I'm not sure that I want to stay in school much longer. Some of my friends are dropping out. There's a war going on in Europe and we might soon be over there, too. All the young men will probably be enlisting soon, and I can be of more use working, or learning to be a nurse."

"A nurse! Thelma dear, work for a while, yes, but better you should be on the lookout for a good husband, a good provider. And how are you going to get one if you can't cook?"

"I should hope that whoever I marry - eventually - will love me for myself, and not for the way I cook!" She softened her reply with a smile. She knew the thwack of the wooden spoon and decided not to chance it.

"Well," Eva sighed as she adjusted the flame under the cooking pot, "I sure hope you marry a meat-and-potatoes man!"

"Me, too!" she answered, as she skipped off to get changed.

*

The bedroom door opened gently, and in walked the meat-and-potatoes man.

"How is the little one doing?" Fred asked as he sat down on the bed next to his wife.

"Sleeping like a baby," she said smiling, "How are the boys doing?"

"I gave them some dinner, and now they're watching television. They already finished their homework at your brother's. I'll sit with her for a while. You go have your dinner and watch some TV with the boys."

"I'll have some dinner while I watch with them. I don't want them to feel left out."

A week or so later, Thelma was on the phone with her mother.

"Yes, Mariuch is fine! But how are you doing? Is your cold any better? Fredy told me that you weren't feeling well. Have you called the doctor?" She hadn't seen her mother since coming home from the hospital, out of fear of catching her cold and giving it to the baby.

"Yeah, I called the doctor. He came to see me," she answered slowly. Those were the days when doctors still made house calls.

"And?"

"He wants me to go to the hospital. But I told him 'no'."

"Are you as sick as all that?" Thelma was becoming worried. "Why don't you want to go to the hospital? Our hospital here is very good."

"I have a feeling, Thelma, that if I go into the hospital, the only way that I will leave will be feet first."

Thelma's heart sank. Eva had very strong feelings and premonitions at times. And, indeed, she had told her daughter that her new baby, already past her due date, would not be born until Friday, under the full moon. Friday the thirteenth, as it happened. And that is exactly what took place.

"Now, Ma, we have really good doctors here, and I am sure that they will be able to figure out what is making you sick, and they will take good care of you."

She was not at all sure that her efforts to reassure her mother were successful, or whether her father had insisted that she listen to her doctor's recommendation, but into the hospital she went. And as sure as Eva had correctly predicted the birth date of her newest granddaughter, she had predicted her own fate. She never got to hold the latest addition to Fred and Thelma's brood, nor the two baby girls who would follow in their time, nor the baby boy who would make her son Freddy's family complete.

Beloved by her children, grandchildren, nieces, nephews, and friends galore, Eva Marrone Calogero was no more. She was the quintessential nonna who could cook up a storm, and made all - especially the young ones - welcome. Her "powers" had been sought after by strangers who wanted to know the sex of their unborn child, or by those cursed by the Evil Eye and needed it to be removed. And she was gone.

*

Thelma and her brother Ferdnando, or Fred or Freddy, had been born and raised in the Bronx, New York. The Bronx of the 1920s and 1930s was not as built up as it is today and there were still plenty of green areas available for the children to romp about. It was a time before the proliferation of supermarkets, and residents bought what they needed from the local butcher, greengrocer, baker, etc., as well as from itinerant vendors going door to door. These last sold everything from ice to live eels.

Reminiscing about those days, Thelma would later recount to her daughters how the eel vendor would place the desired quantity of eels into a sack and dispatch them with a firm smack of the sack against the wall of their apartment building. Funny, the things that one remembers from childhood.

Despite what might make it appear to be a time of plenty in those days, the reality was that the nation was in the throes of the Great Depression, and where there were products available, there was not always money with which to buy them, and sometimes the products themselves would be in short supply or unavailable.

Although Thelma's father, Antonio, seemed to have some pretty good connections, he was not always around for days or weeks at a time. And Eva learned well how to manage under these conditions. Thelma was not unaware of the fragility at times of their economic situation and learned by her mother's example: stocking up when things were in abundance and affordable, and making do when they were not. These habits stayed with her throughout her life.

But all was not doom and gloom for young people growing up in the pre-war years. There was good music - great music, from crooners to swing, from the Boswells to the Andrews Sisters, to name but a few. There were movies and dances and roller skating, and more. For Thelma (or TC, as they often called her) and her friends, the fun was going out in groups of young men and women; they rarely paired off. They would often meet up at her apartment before heading out to have fun - the closer to dinner time, the better. Eva made all of them feel welcome, and always served them as generously as current conditions would permit.

"Let's go to the movies tonight, suggested one of her friends. There are a lot of good ones out right now."

"I want to see *Wuthering Heights*," exclaimed Thelma. "I read the book, and I'm dying to see the movie. I mean, Laurence Olivier, after all." (Thelma may not have been super studious, but she loved to read, to escape to other worlds, and to escape the world she was in.)

"He's dreamy," sighed another of her friends. "What do you think, guys?"

"Why not? What have we got to lose?" was the response.

"Twenty-five cents!" quipped another.

"Let's go, then. We can make the 8 pm showing if we hurry. I don't want to miss the coming attractions," TC said. She really hated being late for anything - especially movies. So, after thanking Eva for the meal, the gang headed out.

A couple of hours later, the gang was strolling back towards Thelma's building.

"How romantic!" gushed one of her friends. "To die for love!"

"I don't know," TC replied, "I guess if I hadn't read the book, I would have liked it better. But they left so much out!"

"I didn't like it too much," said another friend, "I can't wait until *Gone with the Wind* comes out!"

"Me, too!" came a chorus of replies.

"I've read that, too," said Thelma, "and I hope they don't mess that up!"

"Clark Gable, Leslie Howard. How bad can it be?" was the response of her friend, who tended to like movies based on the lead actors.

"It's coming out in a few months, so we don't have long to wait. I really wish that someone would make a movie of *Jane Eyre* though. I loved that book, and I would love to see a movie of it," sighed Thelma.

"TC, you read too much! There's a dance on Friday at the high school gym. Are we in, or out?" asked one of the guys.
"In!" It was unanimous.

*

As the US found its way into World War Two, Thelma made good on her decision to leave school. She had been following the commercial course of study, as opposed to college prep, so she had the skills necessary for office work, and she had no difficulty finding a job. Most of the young men she knew were enlisting, and thus her social circle was shrinking. She continued to write to several of them after they shipped out, and she and her friends - anxious to keep up the morale of their brave soldiers - would sometimes go up to the roof of her apartment building and take photos of one another to send to them. They were not exactly sultry photos - more of the carefree and playful variety. Anything to help out with the war effort!

Despite the deprivations of wartime rationing - and somehow Thelma's father could always get his hands on extra ration stamps - it was still a time of swing music, big bands, and "The Boogie Woogie Bugle Boy of Company B". There was still plenty of fun to be had, and Thelma and her friends, all women now, would still go to the movies and dances - but now with soldiers who were in New York on leave.

TC would still immerse herself in books and was happy to see *Jane Eyre* brought to the screen at last. And Orson Welles as Rochester! Now, that was casting! There were some huge omissions and changes to the original, but Thelma found it a very satisfying adaptation, still capturing Jane's brave and indomitable spirit.

"I am no bird, and no net ensnares me." Thelma loved the line in the book where Jane trumpets her independence and it spoke to her at that time in her life. She was working, earning money, helping with the war effort, and enjoying life. She enjoyed the dating scene, such as it was, but she was not ready to settle down to a life of domestic bliss as yet - if "domestic bliss" were even possible! Her parents were hardly an example of that.

"Whenever I have children," she vowed to herself, "I don't ever want them to hear their parents argue. No raised voices." She also vowed not to look for a husband purely to escape her parents' home. There had to be more. She was worth more…

The Literary Apprenticeship of Charlotte, Emily, and Anne Brontë

By Brenda Whipps

"There was no possibility of taking a walk that day." This opening line from *Jane Eyre* is one of the most famous ever written. Just ten ordinary words instantly captivated the literary world in 1847. However, these words were far from ordinary; this novel became an instant literary sensation, and to this day, the novel still has a tight hold over readers with its gripping narrative.

I remember when I was first introduced to the works of the Brontë sisters. My mother was on a brief work break and took a walk in the long shopping mall while an antique show was happening inside. Thinking that I would enjoy them, my thoughtful mother bought me two antique books: *Lorna Doone* by R.D. Blackmore and *Jane Eyre* by Charlotte Brontë. I was a young college student at the time home on summer break when she surprised me with this beautiful 1944 Random House edition of *Jane Eyre*, with its glorious wood-cut engravings. I found myself closely studying the fine detail in these stunning engravings just like the Brontë children did with engravings in the books they read.

I then proceeded to read the famous opening line of this new treasured book. Those ten words were all it took; I was instantly transported to an earlier time and could not close this powerfully moving novel. I read it straight through, barely coming up for air as I devoured it through to the wonderful conclusion.

At one point in the novel, Charlotte's heroine Jane says, "I am no bird and no net ensnares me; I am a free human being with an independent will." The narrative follows her as she bravely forges her own path in life in this brilliant novel of independence. I now have three editions of this book (clearly one is not enough). It was my first introduction to the Brontë sisters and I knew immediately I had to read more.

Emily Brontë's intriguing opening line to her astonishing novel, *Wuthering Heights*, also published in 1847, begins with, "1801. I have just returned from a visit to my landlord — the solitary neighbour that I shall be troubled with." Like Charlotte's book, I was hooked. I then wanted more. Anne Brontë, in her debut novel, *Agnes Grey*, focuses on exploring and exposing the governess trade. This was published alongside Emily's only novel but she then later wrote what is widely considered to be her masterpiece, *The Tenant of Wildfell Hall*. The novel contains another opening line that immediately pulls the reader into the story - "You must go back with me to the autumn of 1827."

I continue to be inspired by the sisters' powerfully moving words found in their literary works and by their spirits of determination, perseverance, and deep courage. I knew I needed to learn more about these brilliant young sisters as despite their brief lives and very limited experiences, they wrote some of the greatest English literature in history. What inspired them and how did this incredible talent first develop? I needed to know and what I learned along the way was as astonishing as their own
novels and poetry.

Their father, Reverend Patrick Brontë, gave his six children a religious as well as a classical education at home with daily lessons in his study at a time when it was deemed unnecessary to educate one's daughters. Unusually, Charlotte, Emily, and Anne, alongside their brother Branwell, had the freedom to read anything they wanted.

The vastness of the wild Yorkshire moorland surrounding the family home provided limitless inspiration and liberty to the children and would help cultivate the genius of Charlotte, Emily and Anne Brontë. Their parsonage home provided a creative and safe refuge for the sisters throughout their lives after the rigours of boarding school, governess, and teaching jobs.

The children had full access to their father's library including poetry, newspapers, magazines, and classic books of literature. One in particular - *Blackwood's* - was most influential to the children. As well as books, the children had toys which helped with the development of their enthusiastic and vivid imaginations and storytelling abilities. There was also tragedy in the siblings' lives with the loss of their mother and two eldest sisters, Maria and Elizabeth.

The remaining four banded together and in an upstairs room in the parsonage which the servants referred to it as the 'children's study' they began their deep immersion in their imaginary worlds. Childhood drawings are still seen on the walls of this small but important room of creative expression where their storytelling and writing first took hold.

One day in 1826 after returning home from a conference in Leeds, Patrick brought home little gifts for his children including toy soldiers for Branwell. The twelve toy soldiers were known as the 'Young Men' and provided much-needed escapism from the loss of their mother and two sisters. The children's rich imaginations helped transform their play into literature; they began writing using a minuscule script in tiny, homemade books that were matchbox-sized and designed for the soldiers to read. This enabled them to share only with each other the secret world they immersed themselves in, as their tiny books were not legible to adult eyes without enlarging them.

As paper was so expensive, the siblings used wallpaper scraps, old sugar bags, and any scraps they could find to create their books. I can just imagine them pleading with the servants for an old sugar bag or delightfully using the backs of advertising that their father brought home or anxiously watching for a parcel wrapped in brown paper to arrive. The sisters, with their newfound sewing skills taught by their Aunt Branwell, used leftover cotton thread from the samplers they worked tirelessly on as young girls. It may be that some of this thread was used by their small but nimble fingers to sew the bindings of their tiny books. The creative process of their juvenilia would become a long apprenticeship that would help the sisters become the brilliant sisters we celebrate and are inspired by today.

The Second Mrs Fred & the Johnson Women. Part II.

Post-war, Thelma was working in the office of a manufacturing company which supplied the military, and others, with power supplies and transformers. The war might be over, but the need was ongoing. She had worked there for a while now, and she enjoyed it. The pay was good and, although she was more of a general office assistant than anything else, she was learning a bit about electricity and power supplies.

One afternoon, a gentleman walked into the office. She had seen him around the plant once or twice before but had never actually spoken with him. He seemed to be a number of years older than she, of average height, with blue eyes framed by horn-rimmed glasses. His dark blond hair was brushed straight back from his high forehead. As always, he was neatly dressed in a shirt and tie.

Good afternoon, Miss," he said (was that a slight accent?). "My name is Fred Johnson and I would like to speak with Mr. —. Is he available?"

"Let me check. I will be right back," she answered, and, turning, she went into Mr. —'s office to inquire. He was indeed available, and she ushered his visitor into the boss's office.

As the door was closing, she could hear her boss saying, "How are you getting on, Fred? Are you adjusting…"

"I know I heard an accent," she mused to herself, maybe I'll ask him about it if I'm still here when he comes out.

Alas, it was past 5 pm when their meeting ended, and Thelma was well on the way home. As she walked to the subway, she kept seeing his face and wondering what his story was. He was very polite and gentlemanly, and he was not wearing a wedding ring, although not all men did. And there was definitely a bit of an accent.

A week or two later, Fred had another appointment with her boss. He arrived a little bit early and as her boss was running a little bit late, she decided to try and find out a little bit about him. Thelma had always been, and always would be, a people-person, and could strike up a conversation with just about anyone.

"Good afternoon, Mr. Johnson - "

"Call me Fred. Please."

"Hello, Fred. My name is Thelma Calogero, but please call me Thelma."

"Nice to meet you, Thelma."

"You, too, Fred. By the way, please don't think I'm nosy, but I detect a bit of an accent when you speak. Are you from New York?"

"Oh, no," he replied with a smile, "I've lived here over twenty years, but I am from Sweden."

"Well, your English is very good." *Well, that was a pathetic thing to say,* she thought.

"Thanks."

Thelma was just about to try to learn a little more about him, when her boss came out of his previous meeting and waved Fred in. With a slight bow, Fred followed their boss into his office.

As Thelma was getting ready to leave for the day, Fred emerged from the inner sanctum. They walked out together. As they exited the building, Fred asked her which direction she was headed.

"I turn right at the corner to catch the subway. Which way do you go?"

"I have to go to my sister's today, so I am going in the opposite direction. But maybe tomorrow after work we can walk to the park and get to know one another," he suggested shyly.

"I'd really like that," answered Thelma. "Until tomorrow, then."

"Until tomorrow." And they each went their separate ways.

When tomorrow came, and they began to learn a little more about each other, she realized that she had finally met her meat-and-potatoes man.

*

What she learned about him that day, and in other meetings to come, was that he had been the eldest of ten children (at that time - there would be two more born later) when he decided to leave his home town of Stenungsund at fifteen years of age. He stowed away on a ship out of Gothenburg bound for New York. Once he was discovered on board, he was given a job in the kitchen. He ended up working on three Atlantic crossings before jumping ship in New York, where he changed his name from Erling Johansson to Fred Johnson.

He had slept rough for a while, with all the dangers that entailed, until he met up with a childhood friend who took him in and recommended that he get his papers in order and learn English, both of which he did. He worked hard to learn all the skills that he could and to establish a life for himself in his new country. That life included a Norwegian wife and, toward the end of 1944, a baby son. His wife having succumbed to postpartum complications, his son was left in the care of one of his sisters, who had also moved to New York and who had a daughter of about the same age.

He was a bright man who, like Thelma, was an avid reader, and who felt that one could learn how to do almost anything by reading about it, and for whom learning was a lifelong pursuit. Fred was also a man of simple tastes and customs and preferred simple, plainly seasoned fare. He was, indeed, her meat-and-potatoes man.

*

Nearly eighteen months after losing her mother, Thelma and

Fred welcomed another baby girl into the family. Like her older brother and sister, she came into this world at over nine pounds - no wee little babes for this family! But unlike her elder siblings, she made her appearance during the sultry days of late July. Although Thelma had not gained as much weight this time (she had finally learned not to "eat for two"), she was finding it quite uncomfortable to lumber about during the heat and humidity of summer and was quite happy to feel the first signs of labour. Knowing that she still had some time before she needed to go to the hospital and that Fred would have his hands full with three children at home, she set about giving the house a quick clean while she waited for him to come home and pick her up.

Coming home from the hospital after the traditional stop to pick up the kids and show off the newborn to her father and her brother's family, the six of them continued up the hill toward home. Unlike the last time a new baby came home, the day was still quite sunny, no precipitation threatened, and the day was hot and humid. The silent winter woods had given way to abundant leafiness, and the tiger lilies were in full bloom along the driveway.

Thelma used her hanky to pat some beads of perspiration from her face as she settled little Susan Eva - whose middle name was in honour of grandmother - into the bassinet. Maria Ellen was not quite ready to move into a bed, so she had been moved, crib and all, into the bedroom next door, to share it with Tony. Paul had recently been given his own room upstairs, and another bedroom was waiting for Tony up there, in anticipation of the time when Maria and Susan would be roommates.

Thelma thought again of her mother, and a wave of sadness came over her. She would have loved to have had her advice about caring for little girls and trying to balance the needs of all her children. But she had had to make do without her sage wisdom and old wives' tales. How she wished that her girls could have known her and that she could have known them!

*

Their early years were spent romping about with their cousins and with the neighbours' kids - of which there were many: climbing trees, walking in the woods, getting into scrapes, learning to swim in the lake, going on family camping trips, ice skating, building snow forts, and having snowball fights. Fred was a hard-working family man, always with some project at hand to improve their home. One winter in the early 1960s, he lined the front lawn of their hilltop home with plastic, flooded it, and created an ice skating rink. Having previously strung coloured lights up the flagpole to give the illusion of an immense hilltop Christmas tree, his family and their friends spent many hours of delightful nighttime skating, lit by the colours of the season, followed by steaming mugs of hot chocolate.

Thelma kept herself very busy, even apart from keeping house and raising four kids. She belonged to the Ladies' Guild of their parish church, as well as the Women's Auxiliary at the local volunteer fire department, marching in parades and helping to raise funds. And she was almost always a room mother for one of her kids' classrooms. When Susan and Maria became Brownie scouts, their troop was so large that it needed a leader and two assistants. Thelma, of course, was one of the assistants.

Her time as a scout leader did not last long, however. For some seven years after Susan was born, Thelma learned that she would be adding to the family once more. Another winter baby, as it turned out. This was happy news for her, as she loved having young ones around her and the girls were growing fast.

The house was beginning to feel a little bit emptier with Paul having finished school and joined the navy. He came home on leave whenever he could, but he was often stationed overseas. The great concern of everyone, however, was that he might be sent to Vietnam, but for now, he was stationed in the Caribbean. And Tony would be finishing high school in a couple of years and would then head off to college.

So, yes, another baby would be most welcome. It would probably be her last chance as she would be thirty-nine when the baby came, and Fred would be fifty-seven. Time to canvass family and friends for a bassinet and crib. Both of these items were generally passed around between friends and relations, so it was a matter of finding which niece or close friend would have them available when her time came.

*

For Susan and Maria, this was the best Christmas present they could imagine. Some of their older cousins had had babies, but the girls had never paid much attention to them as they were too young for them to play with. But this would be different.

When their father came home from work, the girls were very excited, giddy even.

"Why are you two so silly today?" he asked, smiling.

"We are going to have a new brother or sister," they cried, dancing about. "Do you want a boy, or a girl?" they asked.

"I want a healthy baby," he answered. "Come, sit with me until dinner is on the table." The girls went to sit on either arm of the easy chair into which he had settled. They looked up at him with smiling faces. His Susan, his Mariuch. "I am very happy, too, about the new baby, but there is a chance that the new baby might not be healthy. That it might be defective." As good as his English was, there were still times when his word choice could be said to be lacking. This was one of those times.

"Defective?" Maria asked. "Why?"

"Well, Mariuch, your mother and I are older than most parents, and when that is the case, sometimes a baby can be born with problems."

"You mean, like 'seal babies'?" Maria had seen pictures of Thalidomide babies in a newspaper article under the title of "Seal Babies".

"No, no, not like that! But there could be something, and we just have to hope and pray for a healthy little one." This gave the girls something to think about - but not for long as it was almost Christmas time, after all!

*

Saturday morning, the day after New Year's Day, Thelma was awakened by the first twinges of labour. A glance out her window revealed a snowy panorama, with more flakes starting to fall. After a quick call to the doctor, it was decided that it would be best to head out to the hospital right away and not take any chances with the weather.

Fred hastened upstairs to wake up the fifteen-year-old Tony, who was given the task of taking care of his sisters. He stumbled out of bed and came downstairs. Other than the early hour, he was not entirely displeased with the opportunity to boss his sisters about.

It was a dark-ish day, and the snow flew thick and fast as Saturday morning cartoon shows gave way to old movies in the afternoon. It was too snowy for the kids to go outside and play, and the girls became restless, awaiting news of their new sibling.

Finally, sometime after 4 pm, the girls heard the phone ring and came running into the kitchen where Tony was just hanging up.

"There's been a disaster," he told them, their faces dropping in fear, "It's a girl!"

*

Debbie was their living doll and her sisters doted on her. Born via emergency C-section, and blue from a collapsed lung, a priest was called in the next day to baptize her - just in case. To be safe, mother and daughter had stayed in the hospital for nearly a week, but now they were snugly situated at home, with a new space heater in the bedroom to give her extra protection from the cold of January. Another innovation was the new bathroom which Fred had added to their bedroom. The new family of seven would no longer have to share one bathroom.

Not too long after Debbie's homecoming, their father sat the girls down for a talk. Indeed, like his mother-in-law before him, his foreboding had become reality.

"Your little sister is getting stronger every day, but there is something you must know. She is always going to be slow, and she will never develop the same as other children. She has xxxxxxxxx." He had used the word in common usage for Down Syndrome at the time, and it was many years before that word fell out of favour.

"What does that mean? Will she be able to walk and talk?" Maria asked.

"We think so, but it will take her longer to do those things. And her face looks a little different, too," he answered, not entirely certain himself.

"Different? How?"

"Around the eyes and the forehead, mostly," he replied. "Sometimes, parents will put their children away when they are like this, to be raised by some other people in a kind of institution. We will not be doing that. She will always live with us and be raised as normally as possible."

It had never occurred to Susan and Maria that their sister could be "put away". They were speechless at the thought of it. They already loved her very much and were determined that she would be raised by no one but her family. From that moment on, Susan and Maria made an unspoken yet ironclad pact that they would do all they could to help Debbie develop, love her, and cherish her forever. No one was putting their sister away!

*

Nineteen sixty-seven began as all years do, full of promise, hope for the future, and resolutions made, and broken. Cultural changes were afoot, as well. Within months, the Beatles would release "Sgt. Pepper's Lonely Hearts Club Band", followed soon after by the "Summer of Love" in San Francisco. Hippie culture was everywhere, along with bell bottoms and love beads.

Tony was due to graduate from high school soon and head off for college, and Maria had discovered *Jane Eyre* on the recommendation of her fifth-grade English teacher, who declared it her all-time favourite novel. Maria wasted no time getting her hands on a copy. Like her mother, she admired Jane's independence and strong-willed spirit, but in Maria's case, they were traits that she feared that she lacked in herself. She sincerely doubted that she could have acted as bravely as Jane did in setting out to make and control her own destiny.

The biggest hope of the family, however, was that Paul would soon return from his tour of duty in Vietnam. Every week, the newspapers were filled with casualty counts and although Paul was in the Sea Bees (Construction Battalion), there was no guarantee that the fighting would not come to him. But, by the end of May, he was home - safe and sound!

He had heard some of the fighting and seen some Viet Cong prisoners pass through his camp, but he was never very near the front lines. He was now discharged from active duty and ready to start moving forward. And move, he did, becoming engaged six weeks after coming home, and married before the end of the year.

The family went on vacation to Cape Cod that summer, not camping this time, but staying in a housekeeping cottage. This was the first time that Susan and Maria had wet their feet in the ocean, and the cold saltiness of it did not impress either one of them, although they did enjoy the sand dunes. Paul had stayed behind to go to work, but for the rest of the family, it was expected that this would be their last family vacation, what with Tony soon heading off to college and Paul being married a couple of months after that.

Tony won't be going very far, just three hours away in Boston Thelma reflected. *And Paul will be living nearby once they're married, but the nest is emptying out, little by little. At least we still have a few more years before the girls start to spread their wings.*

*

With Tony soon settled at the university, and Paul about to be married, Thelma and Fred decided to make some alterations to the house so that Debbie, now two years old, could move out of her parents' room and in with her sisters. To this end Fred spent an entire Sunday, with Paul's help, tearing down the walls of the enclosed porch, to build new, insulated walls and then open up the girls' bedroom into this new space, where Debbie could sleep. They finished the day with the exterior walls gone, and the roof held up by wooden supports. They expected to be able to enclose the area by the next weekend at the latest before the autumn days could turn much colder.

The next day, the girls were watching TV, having finished their steak and baked potato dinner. The phone rang in the kitchen. Soon after it stopped, a commercial came on, and Maria took the opportunity to go into the kitchen for a drink of water. The kitchen was dark, except for the light over the sink, but Maria could still see her mother's birthday flowers from ten days ago in the white milk glass vase. On the stove was a portion of steak, still in the frying pan, and a lone baked potato. Thelma was standing at the sink, staring out of the window and smoking a cigarette.

"That was the police," she told her oldest daughter.

"Your father is dead." Maria was so shocked that she couldn't think of a single question to ask. All she could do was mumble that she would tell Susan and return to the living room.

"Susan, the police just called to tell Mom that Dad is dead," she said, almost mechanically. Susan looked as shocked as Maria had, too shocked even for tears, but her elder sister cautioned her. "We mustn't cry now, we don't want Debbie to get upset, we have to be calm."

Before too long, the house was anything but calm as Thelma had called her closest friends and her brother, and people began to arrive. It was all the girls could do to stay calm and out of the way amid the hubbub. The girls went to bed a little later than usual that night - there was no thought of them going to school the next day - and before turning out their light, Thelma kissed each of them and said "I hope you both know that your father loved you very much."

A massive heart attack had carried him away at the age of sixty, in those days before coronary bypass surgery. A full day of structural demolition had taken its toll. The ultimate family man had passed away as a consequence of doing what he could to make the family home more comfortable for all.

Fred's friends and colleagues rallied around the stricken family and finished the job he had begun before the winter weather could set in. Within two months of his passing, Paul and his fiancée were duly married. With Tony away in Boston, where he would live for the next ten years, it had become a house of women. The Johnson Women.

Mapping Emily and Anne Brontë's Fantasy Islands of Gondal and Gaaldine

By Tom Ashworth

Most readers will know the Brontë sisters from their two most famous novels, *Jane Eyre* by Charlotte Brontë and *Wuthering Heights* by Emily Brontë. Literature lovers may also be aware of the novels of their overlooked sister Anne, Charlotte's later novels, and perhaps some of their poems. But far less known is the fact that they were all prolific writers before a single novel or poem had been published, or that their brother Branwell played a key role in their early writings, with stories set in fully-realised imaginary realms, created long before fantasy became the popular genre of today.

As part of their childhood games, the young Brontës conjured up a fanciful version of colonial West Africa where each of the siblings controlled a kingdom with their own capital cities (see Branwell's map below). The siblings wrote their stories in tiny, hand-made booklets, and the setting grew in complexity as the children matured. When the two junior sisters, Emily and Anne, were teenagers they moved on to invent new kingdoms on the imaginary Pacific islands of Gondal and Gaaldine, while the elder brother and sister, Branwell and Charlotte, created a new African kingdom called Angria to the east of Glass Town.

Emily seems to have "stuck by the rascals" who inhabited her internal world until the year of her death.[1] The siblings' young imaginations were fired by stories they had read or heard, including tales about genies, colonial exploits, the Napoleonic wars, the works of Walter Scott, and many others;[2] Emily especially was inspired by Scott's Highland clans which influenced the landscape, politics, and wars of her island of Gondal which she created with Anne.

Within the games, the fictionalised West Africa was discovered by "the twelve young men" based on a set of toy soldiers, who sailed to the land of the Ashantee tribes by the river Niger and established colonies called the Glass Towns.[3] These games were led by the elder children Branwell and Charlotte, with Emily and Anne apparently relegated to secondary roles. It's likely that the younger sisters had some creative tension with their siblings and seemed to enjoy inventing more sombre settings within the Glass Town game. This tension is amply demonstrated in a piece written by Charlotte when she was 14 and Emily was 12; in this story, Charlotte's character Charles Wellesley visits Emily's Glass Town and is highly unimpressed by the down-to-earth country inspired by Yorkshire, with its rows of square houses and factories, where even the nobility eat plain meals of roast beef, Yorkshire puddings and mashed potatoes. Charlotte ends with the damning conclusion "I found my visit intolerably dull—as much so as, I fear, the reader will find this account of it."[4]

This state of affairs clearly wouldn't do for Emily and Anne, who might have started drifting away from the Glass Town setting when Charlotte was away at Miss Wooler's School at Roe Head, starting in January 1831, three months after writing her satire about Emily's Glass Town.[5]

Unfortunately, none of Emily and Anne's writings survives from this early period, so we don't know exactly when or how their new setting was created. But in 1834 we find the briefest mention of their new islands in a diary entry: "The Gondals are discovering the interior of Gaaldine",[6] these "Gondals" are the inhabitants of "a large island in the north Pacific" who seem to be having colonial adventures in deepest Gaaldine, "a large island, newly discovered in the south Pacific".[7]

From 1834 onwards, there are many poems and a few diaries and notes about a great drama unfolding against the backdrop of Gondal's snowy mountains and Gaaldine's tropical palm trees. Emily and Anne both mention prose stories in their diaries, including "a work on the First Wars"[8] and "Emperor Julius's Life",[9] which sadly don't survive, leaving us with only fragments that, nevertheless, allow us to dimly see a dark tale filled with gothic prisons, betrayals, devastating wars, and dramatic landscapes. Several poems are signed by fictional Gondal characters, the most frequent being A.G.A. (Augusta G. Almeda), a raven-haired anti-heroine who is haunted by departed companions, she inspires a cult-like devotion from her followers and appears to become the queen of Gondal, only to be brutally assassinated by one of her spurned lovers.[10] This article focuses on the geography and themes, but anyone interested in a speculative reconstruction of the story should read *Gondal's Queen* by Fannie E. Ratchford.

The Brontës' interest in Scotland began early, as we can see from a piece by their brother Branwell describing their fantasy African kingdoms in the game of the Glass Towns before Gondal had been created. Branwell tells us that Emily and Anne's Glass Town kings were Scots who brought cohorts of settlers from their native land. Branwell's own king was also a Scot who colonised a snowy, heath-bound mountain-scape with a band of highlanders, highly reminiscent of the later Gondal setting.

In contrast, Charlotte's king was the Anglo-Irish Arthur Wellesley (based on the Duke of Wellington's son) who brought Irish settlers to his kingdom.[11] Later, in Emily and Anne's land of Gondal, outlaw bands roam the mountainous highland heath, recalling the Scottish Highland clans featured in the Waverly novels of Walter Scott, who the Brontës read and admired.[12] The below extract from a highlander song in Scott's novel *Waverly* includes the image of the sun illuminating the mountain peaks, later used by Emily in her poem discussed below:

But the dark hours of night and of slumber are past,
The morn on our mountains is dawning at last;
Glenaladale's peaks are illumined with rays,

And the streams of Glenfinnan leap bright in the blaze.

Walter Scott's Highland names like Glenaladale are echoed in the name of the Gondal family of Gleneden (see below) who are involved in a conflict against tyranny, as are the characters in Anne's poems discussed below. Scott's longer narrative poetry was also likely an inspiration, for example, Emily's description of ferns as mourners (below) finds an earlier parallel in Scott's *Lay of the Last Minstrel*, Canto V, stanza I, where the landscape acts as a mourner for the deceased minstrel:

Who say, tall cliff, and cavern lone,
For the departed bard make moan;
That mountains weep in crystal rill;
That flowers in tears of balm distil;
Through his loved groves that breezes sigh,
And oaks, in deeper groan, reply;
And rivers teach their rushing wave
To murmur dirges round his grave.[13]

Another source of inspiration was Shakespeare, especially the historical plays with their political machinations, betrayals, and love affairs. For example, the ambitious and treacherous queen Augusta G. Almeda dreams of being haunted by the shades of people she's wronged, recalling the villainous Richard III's dream in which he is visited by the ghosts of his victims.[14]

Several Gondal characters share names with Shakespeare's, such as Douglas, the assassin of queen A.G.A, possibly named after the Earl of Douglas who rebels against his king in Henry IV, Part 2.[15] This is supported by the influence Shakespeare had on the Glass Town characters created by Charlotte and Branwell, such as the seditious Alexander Percy, Earl of Northangerland, partly inspired by Shakespeare's rebel Henry Percy, Earl of Northumberland in

Henry IV, Parts 1 and 2.

Despite being placed in the North Pacific, Gondal does not resemble a Pacific island in the slightest, the many descriptions of nature in the poems reveal a country very much inspired by Scotland. Much of the landscape is taken up by snowy, mountainous highlands cut by lakes and populated with eagles, deer, and moorcocks, which Emily utilises to both celebrate the beauty of nature and to reflect and contrast with the emotional world of the characters. This is amply demonstrated by the below lines in which Augusta G. Almeda mourns a departed lover called Elbë, who is buried among the mountains:

Bright moon – dear moon! when years have passed
My weary feet return at last –
And still upon Lake Elnor's breast
Thy solemn rays serenely rest
And still the Fern-leaves sighing wave
Like mourners over Elbë's grave
...
Not oft these mountains feel the shine
Of such a day – as fading then,
Cast from its fount of gold divine
A last smile on the heathery plain
And kissed the far-off peaks of snow
That gleaming on the horizon shone
As if in summer's warmest glow
Stern winter claimed a loftier throne –
And there he lay among the bloom
His red blood dyed a deeper hue
Shuddering to feel the ghostly gloom
That coming Death around him threw –[16]

The landscape here is presented as impressive in itself while also representing the deeply conflicted memories and emotions playing through the mourner's mind: the serene lake reflecting the moonlight is the body of Elbë, the departed lover, lying serenely in death as a reflection of his past; he is surrounded by a sea of ferns which act as mourners, who sigh and waver over his grave. A change of rhyme scheme from aabb to abab signals a change of focus: now the speaker is mentally receding to the actual moment of Elbë's death, lit by the setting sun.

This second phase starts with the gentle image of golden light on the mountains, moving up to the ice-covered peaks then abruptly stating "Stern winter claimed a loftier throne –", meaning that no matter how golden and glorious Elbë's life was, death still rules from its cold summit. Here the "bloom" is both the golden sunset and Elbë's red blood which is an even "deeper hue" as the evening light changes from gold to red, again using the image of death gaining precedence over "golden" life, along with the pun of "dyed" meaning "died". This was a violent death, and it ends with a last violent shudder as Death throws a final gloom over Elbë, still recalling the landscape as night's gloom is thrown over the mountains by the sunset. The poetic meter of iambic tetrameter, one of Emily's favourites, gives the poem a fast-paced and song-like rhythm, rushing through the turmoil of traumatic memories to the inevitable end.

This intimate connection between the landscape and the intensity of human experience reoccurs in Emily's novel *Wuthering Heights* in which Catherine Earnshaw's love for Heathcliff and the fate of her soul are tied directly to the surrounding moors.[17] In the novel, the younger Catherine's walk among the local crags strongly recalls the poem just discussed, with its image of the setting sun illuminating the peaks:

"And what are those golden rocks like, when you stand under them?" she once asked.
The abrupt descent of Penistone Craggs particularly attracted her notice, especially when the setting sun shone on it and

the topmost Heights, and the whole extent of landscape beside lay in shadow.

I explained that they were bare masses of stone, with hardly enough earth in their clefts to nourish a stunted tree.

"And why are they bright so long after it is evening here?" she pursued.

"Because they are a great deal higher up than we are," replied I; "you could not climb them, they are too high and steep. In winter the frost is always there before it comes to us; and, deep into summer, I have found snow under that black hollow on the north-east side!"[18]

The golden light on the height of the rocks and hidden winter frost in the black hollow bring to mind the pleasant, sheltered life of young Catherine, which can't keep away the hidden, cold machinations of Heathcliff, who later makes her his captive. Heathcliff, as his name suggests, is intimately tied to the wild landscape throughout the novel, a development of the theme in the poems.

Anne also utilises the wild mountains of Gondal, such as in a pair of poems in which a group of victorious rebels hunt down their defeated enemies, and toast their victory over tyranny (as they see it). But this is a bittersweet celebration for one speaker who looks back with fondness on the freedom of the outlaw life which they have exchanged for becoming tyrants themselves. Here, the mountains are synonymous with the liberty the rebels fought for and the purity of their cause. Paradoxically, victory has ended that very freedom as they leave the free mountains to occupy their enemies' "princely homes", and the two poems hint that the purity of their freedom-fighting has been stained by the brutal chase and slaughter of former oppressors, their roles now reversed:

We have their princely homes, and they
To our wild haunts are chased away,
Dark woods, and desert caves.

And we can range from hill to hill,
And chase our vanquished victors still;
Small respite will they find until
They slumber in their graves.

But I would rather be the hare,
That crouching in its shelter lair
Must start at every sound;
That forced from cornfields waving wide
Is driven to seek the bare hillside,
Or in the tangled copse to hide,
Than be the hunter's hound.[19]

And in a sequel poem written the following day:

But I would rather press the mountain heath,
With naught to shield me from the starry sky,
And dream of yet untasted victory –
A distant hope – and feel that I am free!
...
Is this the end we struggled to obtain?
O for the wandering Outlaw's life again![20]

Anne's outlaw poems present a strong binary: living in the wild landscape is freedom while stately halls and lordship are oppression, this contrasts with Emily's poem where peace and violence, nature and humanity are inextricably intertwined. Anne also uses a strong theme of the intense purity of the struggling life of an outlaw and portrays the violent conflict as a game hunt which doesn't end just because one side has achieved its goals, rather the two factions switch places and the game continues until all are dead, calling into question the purpose of the game itself. This finds a close echo in the later thought of political theorist Hannah Arend who wrote the following about the Great Game, a colonial conflict fought between Britain and Russia over Central Asia:

Playing the Great Game, a man may feel as though he lives the only life worthwhile because he has been stripped of everything which may still be considered to be an accessory. Life itself seems to be left, in a fantastically intensified purity [...] 'When every one is dead the Great Game is finished. Not before.' When one is dead, life is finished, not before, not when one happens to achieve whatever he may have wanted. That the game has no ultimate purpose makes it so dangerously similar to life itself.[21]

The Great Game in Afghanistan began and escalated at the exact time Emily and Anne were developing their own colonial conflicts in the 1830s and '40s,[22] and their brother Branwell wrote a poem about the Afghan War as it was happening, which was published in a local newspaper.[23]

While it's impossible to say whether Emily and Anne were inspired by contemporary events in central Asia, this still shows that they were touching on contemporary themes of freedom, colonialism, and bare human experience which are applicable well beyond the fiction of Gondal. It's clear that this wasn't just childish escapism.

Similarly to Anne's poem, we find a character of Emily's, called R. Gleneden, dismayed after a military victory, in this case he is mourning his brother who has died in the conflict:

One is absent, and for one
Cheerless, chill is our hearthstone –
One is absent, and for him
Cheeks are pale and eyes are dim –

Arthur, brother, Gondal's shore
Rested from the battle's roar –
Arthur, brother, we returned
Back to Desmond lost and mourned:

Thou didst purchase by thy fall

Home for us and peace for all;
Yet, how darkly dawned that day –
Dreadful was the price to pay!
...
Yet the grass before the door
Grows as green in April rain;
And as blithely as of yore
Larks have poured their day-long strain.[24]

Here, the landscape doesn't reflect an inner turmoil, and in fact stands in opposition to it, natural life flourishes in stark contrast to the death hanging over the speaker. The mourner has to confront the incongruity of a world that continues as always, heedless of the tragedy that's devastated their family. The poem goes on to use imagery of a game hunt when R. Gleneden goes bird shooting and, as in Anne's poem, this victorious hunt is equated with the military victory, neither can bring joy to Gleneden because of what's been lost.

Seasonal changes and the passing of time are further features Emily and Anne used to tie the landscape to the characters and story. For example, in a poem about an imprisoned member of the Glenden family who has fought against a tyrant, but was imprisoned during Spring or Summer, and they are now asking their jailor if it has turned to Winter. The jailor replies that Winter has already come and gone, and it is May again:

Tell me, watcher, is it winter?
Say how long my sleep has been?
Have the woods I left so lovely,
Lost their robes of tender green?
...
'Captive, since thou sawest the forest
All its leaves have died away
And another March has woven
Garlands for another May –

'Ice has barred the Arctic water,
Soft south winds have set it free
And once more to deep green valley
Golden flowers might welcome thee' — [25]

    The changing seasons highlight Gleneden's isolation from the outside world as he has lost track of time, a fundamental human experience and a connection to the natural world, meaning he has been stuck in a limbo of mental and physical entrapment. Gleneden goes on to impotently reflect on their compatriots' struggle against a tyrant and dreams of carrying out an assassination, concluding that they have achieved nothing in their struggles.

    The changing of seasons here highlights both the despair and desperate hope; firstly, Winter has indeed come and killed off the leaves of the forest (Gleneden's side), but Spring has come again and life renews, leading to the bittersweet conclusion that Gleneden's struggle has been reborn, but is still the same struggle as before, it hasn't achieved its goals. The intent seems to be that the violent, political machinations of men are cyclical and never-ending, which can be directly compared to Anne's poem about the victorious outlaws above (and Arendt's political commentary): just as the seasons change and return to their beginning, so do the ups and downs of humanity.

    Emily also commented on the violent and cyclical nature of life in an essay she wrote while studying French in Brussels, titled "Le Papillon" (The Butterfly). In the essay, she describes the seemingly hopeless scenario of a violent and sinful world, before introducing the Christian concept of the apocalypse which will sweep away sin with holy fire and usher in a new Heaven and a new Earth.[26] This supernatural understanding of the struggles of life on Earth is, of course, found in the Gondal poems with appropriate natural imagery, such as one in which a young girl persuades her father not to mourn his dead friends because the rest in

the grave means they have sprouted like
seeds into an immortal destiny with God:

You told me this, and yet you sigh,
And murmur that your friends must die.
Ah! my dear father, tell me why?
For, if your former words were true,
How useless would such sorrow be;
As wise, to mourn the seed which grew
Unnoticed on its parent tree,
Because it fell in fertile earth,
And sprang up to a glorious birth –
Struck deep its root, and lifted high
Its green boughs, in the breezy sky.[27]

The image of mortal life as a seed which germinates
into eternal life has Biblical parallels, most strongly recalling 1
Corinthians 15:35-44 where St Paul compares the mortal body
to a wheat seed which sprouts as the imperishable,
resurrected body. This concern with natural, seasonal cycles
re-occurs in *Wuthering Heights*, where the highly precise
passage of time is marked by changing weather and the
appearance of seasonal plants, a topic which has been much
studied,[28] which demonstrates Emily's continued
fascination with the continuum between the natural world
and human society, arenas of both great beauty and violence.

In contrast to Gondal, Emily and Anne sketched the
island of Gaaldine much more loosely in the surviving
writings. The only solid descriptions show us a land with a
tropical climate, populated with rivers, palm trees, cedars and
"prairies bright with flowers",[29] perhaps suggesting
inspiration from Africa, the Americas or the Caribbean, which
were subjects for colonial dispatches in Blackwoods Magazine
which the family is known to have read. In one poem,
Gaaldine functions as a character's childhood "Eden" which
they contrast with the cold, wild winter in Gondal which is

poorly compensated for by Gondal's pleasant Springs. The scenario is a clear representation of idyllic, carefree childhood leading to a loss of innocence in the stormy uncertainties of adulthood:

I thought of many a happy day
Spent in her Eden isle
With my dear comrades, young and gay
All scattered now so far away
But not forgot the while!

Who that has breathed that heavenly air
To northern climes would come
To Gondal's mists and moorlands drear
And sleet and frozen gloom?

Spring brings the swallow and the lark
But what will winter bring?
Its twilight noons and evenings dark
To match the gifts of spring?[30]

It's not a geographical accident that this transition from childhood to adulthood involves a journey across the ocean, as it is a frequent symbol of transition in Emily's poems. The stormy sea is elsewhere used to represent the turbulent life of Augusta G. Almeda, which had transitioned to calm waters before being cut short by her assassination.[31] Elsewhere, death is presented as a journey across the sea to a distant shore,[32] an apt image where the vast ocean is a gulf separating the living from the dead, with the afterlife as the far destination beyond the horizon of those left on earth. The metaphor was used by other authors before Emily[33] and it is possibly a classical allusion, as Odysseus sails across the ocean to the land of the dead in the Odyssey, Book 11.

Gaaldine seems to have been colonised by people from Gondal and had become home to six kingdoms by the time

Anne wrote a list of fictional place names into a geography textbook,[34]. These kingdoms come to be involved in Gondal's wars as there seem to be alliances between Gondal nobles and the monarchs of Gaaldine.[35] Gondal itself may have been settled by explorers from Britain, as the Glass Towns were, although its early history is unclear. One poem mentions the fact that a major character was the first feudal chief of Aspin Castle in Gondal, implying a history of castle building to secure new holdings.[36]

Colonialism and feudalism must have been themes in the prose stories but a detailed analysis is difficult due to the scarcity of the theme in the surviving material. However, attempts have been made by scholars such as Christopher Haywood, who argues that the war poems are based on the history of Irish insurrections against British rule,[37] which may be an overly restrictive interpretation due to the breadth of Emily and Anne's influences.

There is no surviving evidence that either Emily or Anne drew maps of their settings, but several clues indicate that they had a consistent, detailed geography. The most obvious examples are nine Gondal and Gaaldine place names written by Anne in a dictionary of geography owned by the family, several of these locations appear in the poems, including a place called "Ula" described as "a kingdom in Gaaldine, governed by 4 Sovereigns."[38] It has long been noted that Emily created highly consistent geography for the setting of *Wuthering Heights,* along with the precise timeline,[39] suggesting she either drew a map or mentally retained the geography.

Another clue lies in the parallel Glass Town setting of their siblings, for which their brother Branwell drew a full map and wrote detailed geographic and demographic descriptions of its various kingdoms. Because much of Emily and Anne's material has been lost, it's possible they created similar maps or descriptions, although it's also possible these details were kept in their heads, only coming out in the writing process.

Both the emotional and physical geography of Gondal and Gaaldine were outpourings of Emily and Anne Brontë's creativity, unconstrained by thoughts of publication, which give us a fascinating insight into their creative process that blended natural history, literature, and theology. The poems in particular show us creators who could write in the voices of multiple characters with very different relationships to the natural landscape, which itself is presented as a multi-faceted world that can't be boiled down to single meaning. The lost prose stories may well have explored this complex of world views in greater detail, which make their loss all the more keenly felt.

ৡৡৡ

[1] Christine Alexander (ed.) *The Brontës: Tales of Glass Town, Angria, and Gondal.* Oxford: Oxford University Press, 2010, p. xxxix

[2] Heather Glen (ed.) *Charlotte Brontë: Tales of Angria.* London: Penguin, 2006, p. liii

[3] Alexander, *Tales of Glass Town*, pp. xiv-xvii

[4] Charlotte Brontë, A Day at Parry's Palace by Lord Charles Wellesley, October 1830 (Alexander, *Tales of Glass Town*, pp. 40-43)

[5] Alexander, *Tales of Glass Town*, pp. xxxiv-xxxvi

[6] Emily and Anne Brontë, Diary Paper, 24 November 1834 (Alexander, *Tales of Glass Town*, p. 485)

[7] Anne Brontë, List of place names noted by Anne in *A Grammar of General Geography, by Revd. J. Goldsmith* (Alexander, *Tales of Glass Town*, p. 494)

[8] Emily Brontë, Diary Paper, 30[31] July 1845 (Alexander, *Tales of Glass Town*, p. 490)

[9] Anne Brontë, Diary Paper, 31 July 1845 (Alexander, *Tales of Glass Town*, p. 492)

[10] Emily Brontë, "Sleep brings no joy to me"; The Death of A.G.A. (Janet Gezari (ed.) *Emily Brontë: The Complete Poems*. London: Penguin, #29, #148)

[11] Branwell Brontë, [Angria and the Angrians] III(e), 31 August 1836 (Neufeldt, *Works of PBB*, vol. 2, p. 654) - Branwell wrote this piece after Emily and Anne had split off to create Gondal, but it describes the earlier history of the Glass Towns when they were still involved.

[12] Charlotte Brontë, Letter to Ellen Nussey, 4 July 1834 (Margaret Smith (ed.) *Charlotte Brontë: Selected Letters*. Oxford: Oxford University Press, p. 5); Juliet Barker. *The Brontës*. 2nd edn. London: Abacus, 2010, p. 318; Jacques Blondel. "Literary Influences on *Wuthering Heights*" [1955] in Miriam Allot (ed.) *Wuthering Heights: A Casebook*. Rev. edn. Houndmills: Macmillan, 1992, pp. 157-8

[13] Their father, Patrick Brontë, bought a copy of *The Lay of the Last Minstrel* to celebrate his graduation from Oxford in 1806, the year after its release. (Barker, *The Brontës*, p. 15)

[14] Emily Brontë, "Sleep brings no joy to me" (Gezari, *EB Poems*, #29), compare *Richard III*, Act V, scene 2. Another connection is that both monarchs are accompanied by a character named Lord Surrey (The Death of A.G.A., line 143 [#148]). A different Lord Surrey fights at the Battle of Flodden in Walter Scott's *Marmion*, Cantos V-VI.

[15] Another possible inspiration is Archibald Douglas, Earl of Angus, in Scott's *Marmion*, Cantos V-VI. However, this Douglas stays loyal to his king, James IV of Scotland.

[16] Emily Brontë, "There shines the moon, at noon of night –" lines 11-14, 25-32 (Gezari, *EB Poems*, #10)

[17] Emily Brontë, *Wuthering Heights*, 1847, chs. I.9, I.12

[18] Emily Brontë, *Wuthering Heights*, 1847, ch. II.4 (=18)

[19] Anne Brontë, "We know where deepest lies the snow", lines 8-21 (Alexander, *Tales of Glass Town*, p. 473)

[20] Anne Brontë, "Come to the banquet – triumph in your songs!" lines 21-30, 35-36 (Alexander, *Tales of Glass Town*, pp. 473-4)

[21] Hannah Arendt. *The Origins of Totalitarianism*. New edn. San Diego: Harcourt Brace, 1973, p. 217 (The quote "When every one is dead..." is from Rudyard Kipling's *Kim*)

[22] The beginning of the Great Game is usually dated to 1830. During the Brontës' lifetimes, it lead to the Anglo-Afghan War of 1838-42 and the Anglo-Sikh Wars of 1845-48. (Jonathan L. Lee. *Afghanistan: A History from 1260 to the Present*. London: Reaktion Books, 2018, pp. 193, 225-242, 306)

[23] Branwell Brontë, The Affgan War, published in the Leeds Intelligencer 7 May 1842 (Victor Neufeldt (ed.) *The Works of Patrick Branwell Brontë*. New York: Garland, vol. 3, p. 367)

[24] Emily Brontë, "From our evening fireside now", lines 17-28, 5-8 (Gezari, *EB Poems*, #81)

[25] Emily Brontë, Gleneden's Dream, lines 1-4, 9-16 (Gezari, *EB Poems*, #49)

[26] Emily Brontë, Le Papillon (The Butterfly), 11 August 1842 (Sue Lonoff (ed.) *The Belgian Essays*. New Haven: Yale University Press, 1997, pp. 176-92; Translation available online: http://pioneer.chula.ac.th/~pukrit/bba/butterfly.pdf)

[27] Emily Brontë, Faith and Despondency, lines 42-52 (Gezari, *EB Poems*, #i[153])

[28] C.P. Sanger, "Remarkable Symmetry in a Tempestuous Book" [1926] in Allot, *WH Casebook*, pp. 109-117; S.A. Power. The Chronology of "Wuthering Heights". *Brontë Society Transactions*, 16:2, 1972, pp. 139-143; A. Stuart Daley. A Revised Chronology of Wuthering Heights. *Brontë Society Transactions*. 21:5, 1995, pp. 169-173; Michael Weber. *Timelines in Emily Brontë's Wuthering Heights*. Trans. Catherine Campbell. Frankfurt: Peter Lang, 2020

[29] Emily Brontë, Geraldine, line 9 (Gezari, *EB Poems*, #125); M.G. for the U.S., lines 11-12 (#142)

[30] Emily Brontë, M.G. for the U.S., lines 13-25 (#142)

[31] Emily Brontë, The Death of A.G.A., lines 335-8 (Gezari, *EB Poems*, #148)

[32] Emily Brontë, "I die but when the grave shall press", lines 5-8 (Gezari, EB Poems, #34); "Where beams the sun the brightest", lines 21-24 (#146); Faith and Despondency, lines 53-62 (#i[153])

[33] Janet Gezari. *Last Things*. Oxford: Oxford University Press, 2007, p. 47; see Isaac Watts (1674-1748) A Prospect of Heaven Makes Death Easy, lines 7-8, 13-16: "Death like a narrow sea divides/ This heavenly land from ours.", "But timorous mortals start and shrink/ To cross this narrow sea,/ And linger shivering on the brink,/ And fear to launch away."

[34]Anne Brontë, List of place names noted by Anne in *A Grammar of General Geography, by Revd. J. Goldsmith* (Alexander, *Tales of Glass Town*, p. 494)

എഎഎ

The Second Mrs Fred & the Johnson Women. Part III.

By Maria Johnson

Thrust into a situation that she had not anticipated, after nearly twenty years of marriage to a loving and caring husband and father; a solid working-class man who took care of all of his family's needs and wants while still sending charitable donations almost weekly, Thelma found herself a widow at forty-two. Shew had three minor children at home - the oldest of which was just eleven - and was not at all sure how, or if, she would be able to make ends meet.

The life lessons of her mother were not lost on her. She had been through the Great Depression, she would get through this. She banked the life insurance payout against emergencies. She began to receive survivors' benefits from the government - for herself and four children (Tony was eligible as he was in university). She and Fred had always planned to help each child with college expenses, but now that was out of the question.

What did Eva do when money was scarce and her husband was off gallivanting? She had no "marketable skills", although some folks would slip her some money for taking off the Evil Eye. How had she managed?

Thelma hadn't worked since getting married and, besides, she had a two-year-old with Down Syndrome. She wasn't even walking yet, although that was because she didn't need to as everyone was happy to carry her around. When she did walk, at three, she was so good at it that it was obvious that she had been taking advantage of the situation and only pretending not to be able to walk. Debbie was still too young for the available pre-school programme, so going out to work was out of the question.

Thelma racked her brains trying to come up with a solution. Maybe she could sell something? Just as Jane Eyre had tried to sell her gloves for some bread, Thelma knew what she had to do. Fred had bought himself a brand new, bright red Ford sedan over the summer. The car loan included credit life insurance. He had made but one payment, but the insurance came into play, the car loan was paid off, and she sold the car.

There was a small mortgage on the house, a loan taken to finance recent home improvements. The house had about three acres of land attached. She sold one acre and held the mortgage, thus covering her mortgage expenses.

Eventually, though, Thelma did have to go out to work part-time. Debbie was by then in pre-school, and a neighbour took care of her until the girls came home from school and she could be cared for by her sisters. She enjoyed her work at the department store and made good use of her employee discount. This, combined with the fact that Maria had taken a sewing course the summer before her father died and could make much of her own clothes, meant that she could clothe her children inexpensively.

At some point, though, Thelma learned that her male colleagues had a higher hourly wage than she did. She wasn't happy about it, but tried to justify it by telling Maria that she understood why they got more money - they were family men. Of course, Maria didn't need to point out to her mother that she was a family woman. It was just the way things were back then, and people of Thelma's generation didn't often question it.

One day, Thelma asked Maria to get something out of her wallet for her. While looking for the desired item, she found a charge card for a local department store. The name embossed on the card was "Mrs Fred Johnson". Maria was quite taken aback. Not only was "Mr Fred Johnson" no longer alive, but her mother was not even the only wife he had had. His first wife had been "Mrs Fred Johnson". Anybody could have been known as "Mrs Fred Johnson". Her mother was the second "Mrs Fred Johnson."

The social convention in those days was to refer to a married couple as Mr and Mrs John Doe, which had always grated on Maria's nerves. Why must a woman lose her identity just because she was married? But to women of her mother's age, it was the status quo and, even at this enlightened time, a married woman could not open a charge card without her husband's consent. It was different for widows, though, and as long as she could meet the underwriting requirements, she could obtain credit and enter into contracts on her own.

Eventually, Thelma left the department store job and took a job driving special education students to and from school, including Debbie. She was offered the job because the drivers on staff could never get up the hill to the house, and she was an expert at it.

With Susan and Maria striking out on their own, Thelma came to the difficult decision to sell the family home and move into a townhouse condo. The house that Fred had so lovingly built and transformed and had literally died for was just too much work for her alone with Debbie, so the move was made.

But what of Susan and Maria? From the time that their father had died and their brothers left, they had forged an ever deeper bond between them, dedicated to protecting and nurturing Debbie, and helping their mother when needed. Both of them had read *Jane Eyre* and Mrs Gaskell's biography of Charlotte Brontë, and began referring to themselves as "genii". Inspired by the fictional Jane's independence, they would each forge their own paths, rarely in the way that any of them would have foreseen, but they did it their way.

But not only were they "genii" in their own minds - they were the Johnson Women. Susan and Maria had a motto; "Never underestimate the power of the Johnson Women." Their father gone and their brothers out of the picture, Susan, Maria, and Debbie had had shared experiences, struggles, and triumphs to which their brothers had not been a party. Their struggles - and bond - were something of which their brothers had no part.

Eventually, Thelma left the transportation job, obtained her equivalency diploma, and began to work as a paraprofessional in special education at the middle school level - a job which she loved, and which gave her much personal satisfaction. Debbie graduated high school and was working in a sheltered environment administered by an advocacy agency. She was very proud to be a "breadwinner", happily signing her name on the back of her paychecks. Susan spurned the chance to study art directly after high school, preferring to work at a variety of jobs until she felt the time was right to continue her studies. She obtained her bachelor's degree in her forties, and went on to earn two master's degrees as well.

What of Maria? The most timid, complacent, and unassertive of Thelma and Fred's offspring, she spent many years after college working and dedicating much of her free time to Thelma and Debbie. She was content living in her home town and could never envision leaving - until she met someone who convinced her to give up the life she had known heretofore and embark on an international adventure. She, who had envied Charlotte Brontë's plan to go to Brussels - into the unknown - but was fearful of doing anything along those lines, did exactly that. But that is a tale for another time.

Contributors to this Edition

Nicola Friar is a writer, editor, and blogger. She is the author of *A Tale of Two Glass Towns* and has edited four Brontë themed collections to date. Her main interest is the lives and works of the Brontë family; she makes regular visits to their former home - the village of Haworth - and runs a Brontë themed book club. You can connect with her on Twitter and Instagram under the handle @BronteBabeBlog, or over at www.facebook.com/BronteBabeBlog

Jess Tubby is an artist who works mainly in her precious spare time when she isn't looking after several small humans and animals. You can find her on Instagram under the handle @TubbyInks where she displays her work.

Karen Arthur Neis is the illustrator and author of *Abul-Abbas The Elephant*, a children's book about Charlemagne's elephant. They also created the covers of the four "Rock-and-Roll Brontë" novels, and illustrated *The Frankenstein of the Apple Crate*, a children's book about young Mary Shelley. Their illustrations have been featured in the e-zines *Enchanted Conversations* and *Headcanon* Magazine. They live in Southern California.

Maria van Mastrigt has been a Charlotte Brontë fan since reading *Jane Eyre* when she was eleven years old. However, her passion for the Brontë family and their history started some ten years later, when she discovered the sisters' other novels and Mrs Gaskell's biography of Charlotte. She later moved to Haworth and worked at the museum for a number of years.

Debs Green-Jones is an artist, illustrator, and amateur poet who has a slight obsession with the Brontë family.

Alice Harling is an aspiring Brontë scholar from Huddersfield. She is currently pursuing her PhD in English Literature at the Chinese University of Hong Kong.

Naomi B. is a Brontë fan and writer who was born in the middle of a decade during which people were wearing cool high waist jeans and listening to Nirvana or The Cranberries. Her poetry collection *Gold* was released in 2022.

Tracy Neis is the author of the "Rock-and-Roll-Brontës" series of novels (*Mr. R*, *Restless Spirits*, *Wildfell Summer*, and *Nowhere Girl*), adaptations of Brontë sisters' stories with a modern, British Invasion-era twist. Tracy has also written a YA collective biography of African American poets, and a short play about The Beatles that was performed as part of the 2021 Liverpool Fringe Festival. She lives in Southern California.

Rebekah Clayton grew up a Brontë-loving, velvet-clad, herb-gardening nerdette in post-punk London (loved that eyeliner). She soon escaped to the wild moors of Derbyshire to seek out lapwings, elf-bolts, and inspiration. She is a published author and poet.

Tess Bentley lives with her husband and four sons in the foothills of the Sierra Nevadas with their recue cat, Patch. When she's not writing historical fiction, you will find her with a Brontë book in one hand and probably a cup of coffee in the other. Her debut novel *Vale* is due to be published in 2023.

Katrina Reilly is a school librarian, former teacher, and magazine columnist. She loves the Brontës, travelling, and old movies. She is currently writing her first novel.

Emmeline Burdett t is a writer, translator and academic who lives in London. She is a co-editor of the blog journal *Public*

Disability History.

Maria Johnson was born and raised in Danbury, CT, USA, and became a Brontë lover at the age of ten when a teacher recommended that she read Jane Eyre. When she moved to Latin America at the age of thirty-six, her Brontë library went with her, a loyal companion through twenty-six years and six international moves. Now back in the US, it continues to expand as does her involvement with all things Brontë. Since returning home, and experiencing lockdown restrictions, she has finally begun to do what she has threatened for so many years – write!

Brenda Whipps is a long-time Brontë fan.

Tom Ashworth is a Brontë fan who particularly enjoys the Brontë juvenilia.

Printed in Great Britain
by Amazon

31330294R00086